Something Sisters

31 Day Devotional

Elaine Kennelly

WESTBOW
PRESS
A DIVISION OF THOMAS NELSON

WestBow Press books may be ordered through booksellers or by contacting:

WestBow Press
A Division of Thomas Nelson
1663 Liberty Drive
Bloomington, IN 47403
www.westbowpress.com
1-(866) 928-1240

Cover design created by SiteSell.com

ISBN: 978-1-4497-7150-8 (e)
ISBN: 978-1-4497-7151-5 (sc)

Library of Congress Control Number: 2012919227

Printed in the United States of America

WestBow Press rev. date: 2/18/2013

Contents

Something Sisters
31 Day
Devotional

On the
Path of Life,
Every Woman
Needs a
Something Sister!

I dedicate this book to
my husband, Tom, the love
of my life.
For all that we've been through,
I give this book with love to you.

Let us run with endurance
the race God has set before us.
We do this by keeping our eyes on
Jesus
the Champion who initiates
and perfects our faith.
(Hebrews 12: 1b–2 NLT)

List of Illustrations

Introduction

*H*ave you ever had a crazy idea pop into your head?

That's what happened to my husband, Tom. He had the formidable task of announcing the entertaining dancing duo, Barb and Elaine, at our housewarming party. "And now, ladies and gentlemen, here are the Something Sisters, because they are really *something*!"

Twenty years have passed, but the Something Sisters were born that night in our new house in West Bend, Wisconsin.

Then one day I abbreviated Something Sisters in a card I sent to Barb, putting the SS together. It looked like a path to me, so I wrote to her, "On the Path of Life, Every Woman Needs a Something Sister."

Twenty years have passed, and we are still best friends, because that is what a Something Sister is—a best friend.

Barb, thank you for all the memorable, fun, and crazy times we have shared for forty-five years! Those memories are mostly delightful; some are devastating, such as when Matthew died. But they are always consistently faithful and abounding in a love only two special friends can share.

I want the world to know there could not be a better "sister" than Barbara Harriman. Barb, you have proven this to be true: "A friend loves at all times."

Marnie Smith, you are a treasure I will always appreciate. When others forgot, you remembered. When others drifted away, you drew near. When others said nothing, you comforted and you called. You brought laughter at a time when there was only sadness and despair. What a blessing from God you have been to me for over forty years! You have proven this to be true: "Love never fails."

If you have a best friend sister, you know what I feel in my heart now. You feel loved, affirmed, treasured, and appreciated. As we are maturing in age on our path of life, it is now more important than ever to celebrate our long-lasting friendships, our best friends.

When you give this book to your Something Sister, put her name in all the blanks provided, and if you have your own copy, put your name in the blanks. My desire is for this book to be personalized and used over and over and over. It really becomes a part of you and your day.

We never forgot that instant introduction of Tom's, because God planted a seed that night, and He allowed it to take root through the years. God has blessed that little root, and it has grown, ever so slowly but ever so consistently.

For the past two years, I have been praying to God, asking Him to use me in the last quadrant of my life. "Papa, give me something so big it would be way over my head, and God alone would get all the credit, thanks, and glory. Or Papa, something so small I would be content to do nothing but give You all the credit, thanks, and glory just for life itself."

This quote from Erma Bombeck hangs in my kitchen.

> When I stand before God at the end of my life, I would hope that I would have not a single bit of talent left and could say, "I used everything You gave me."

I took a pen and added these words: "to honor You."

So here is my confession—His answer is "way over my head." This book and website have challenged me every day for the last ten months, and we're not yet finished, as the website continues to grow.

I want to especially thank our youngest son, Nathan, for all the sunshine he provided while growing up. Nate, you were the joy in our home. Where there was struggle with Matthew, there was sparkle and sweetness with you. You also were hurting and grieving the loss of your only sibling, yet your love and positive attitude helped me to persevere through those very sad days. You have since grown into continued joy for Dad and me. I love you and take pride in your many accomplishments, and thank you for bringing your wife, Misty, into our family, where she, too, is loved and appreciated.

As ever, my beloved Tom has been my steady support and encouragement. You see, I have a track record of coming up with great ideas and a vision to accompany them. But guess what? They all take work! My faithful, supportive, and loving husband is forever present to take on the project with me, cheering me on, comforting me at times, but always loving me through it.

Thank you, my precious husband. We have been on an adventure with God together, and we have survived even the tragic death of our son. We have not merely survived but thrived, and what a lovely journey it has been.

Of course, it is the gift of lasting friendship so generously given by all my precious Something Sisters who deserve the accolades for sharing their lives with me. I love each one of you! Thank you for your steadfastness and loyal friendship, which has been a God-given gift to me.

With God's love, compassion, and infinite patience, He has allowed words to pop on a page, and the *Something Sisters 31 Day Devotional* has come to life.

Miraculous!

Day 1
For God so Loved the World

*a*ccording to a report on Worldometers.com by Forrester Research, there were over *one billion PCs in use worldwide* by the end of 2008, with projections of two billion *in use* by 2015. So right now, we're at about 1.5 billion, give or take a few million.

Out of that 1.5 billion, I noticed Google Trends and saw the number-one topic on January 9, 2012, was John 3:16.

Guess what? God is still in control … of people, events, and His Word. God's Word will never return to Him void and empty (Isaiah 55:11). If God says it, it *will* happen!

> For God loved the world so much that He gave His one and only Son, so that everyone who believes in Him will not perish, but have eternal life. (John 3:16 NLT)

Why were millions of people looking up John 3:16 on their computers on Monday, January 9, 2012?

Because there was one person—one football player—who had written John 3:16 under each of his eyes, and that was Tim Tebow, the quarterback for the Denver Broncos at that time. He had just won an extraordinary NFL playoff game, completing a long pass for a touchdown in overtime.

Here's another miracle: I never look to see what the top searches are on Google. Believe me, that would not be on my to-do list. It was a "quirk of the computer," as I like to say, but there it was—John 3:16. I saw it with my own eyeballs!

My dear Something Sisters, John 3:16 is life-changing. If you believe Jesus is the Son of God and that He died for you, to put you back into a right relationship with God, then guess what?

You have eternal life.

You will spend eternity in heaven.

It is a promise from God, and God never breaks a promise!

Maybe you knew about Jesus before you read this, or maybe you were one of the searchers on Google that day. You know what? It doesn't make any difference. God loves you, and He created *you* to be His child.

Here's another great Bible verse.

> How great is the love the Father has lavished on us, that we should be called children of God! And that is what we are! (1 John 3:1)

Something Sister, you are God's child, His daughter. God invites you into His family, and if you RSVP with yes, your life will be changed forever.

Jesus talks about Himself in the gospel of John, chapter 10:

> I tell you the truth. I am the gate for the sheep … whoever enters through Me will be saved … I have come that they may have life, and have it to the full.

The sheep? That's you and me.

According to Gospelcentric.org, David Murray writes, "Sheep are foolish, slow to learn, demanding, stubborn, strong, love to stray, unpredictable, follow mindlessly, are dependent, and extremely restless."

Slow to learn ... follow mindlessly ... stubborn. Yup! That sums it up pretty well.

Remember the movie *Dumb and Dumber*? Well, Tom and I were vacationing at the beautiful white-sand beaches of Alabama. My mother, brother, and sister-in-law joined us.

In the very first hour we were there, my brother, Eric, overcome with the vast beauty of the billowing waves, ran right into the Gulf of Mexico and took a dive, head-first.

Ahhh, what an exhilarating moment!

He came out of the water only to remember he had been wearing his glasses—like in glasses he needed to wear to see everything—with no spare pair in the suitcase. We comforted him with the fact that advertising icon Charlie the Tuna would now have better eyesight.

Then, just a few hours later, Tom, my husband, dove into the swimming pool with his new $400 Smartphone in the pocket of his swimming suit. Oh, yes, the same phone his boss had given to him just the day before to be used while we were vacationing.

My mother, being the funny and clever person she is, dubbed them "Dumb and Dumber," which added to the fun of the whole week. In fact, every once in a while, we still use it! Lovingly, of course.

Notoriously dumb and stubborn, describes our life here on earth without a faith in Jesus Christ. Give your heart to Him and your life will be radically changed. You will know without a doubt that you are in a right relationship with God. You will be a new creation, one with purpose.

The Great Shepherd promises to lead you.

Prayer

Dear Jesus, I need You so much in my life. In fact, I desperately need a shepherd who will care for me and keep me on the right path for my life.

Day by day, You have opened Your arms to welcome me, and I have often walked right past You, thinking I had all the answers I needed for life. But I do not have life to "the full." I am missing out on Your blessings. Just like sheep, I am stubborn.

Today I walk through the gate and enter Your sheepfold with a heart of total repentance and surrender. Please forgive my stubbornness and all of my selfishness.

It is with deep joy and thankfulness that I lift up my face to You, knowing I am your precious daughter, whom You love very much. I am forgiven, and heaven awaits me! John 3:16 is my verse.

In my Savior's loving name I pray. Amen.

The Gospel Poem

You can rest assured in Jesus.

God sees His perfect child in you.

John 3:16 holds salvation's plan,

Because of God, the Word came true.

God so loved the people of the world,

He sent His Son to die upon a cross;

To pay the price for sin and death.

He desires no one to be lost.

The Father did not send His Son

To condemn and bring defeat.

No, He sent His Son to die for us;

Our salvation's now complete.

If you believe Jesus paid the price,

The precious Gospel gift is yours.

God's Holy Spirit now lives in you,

Rejoice! A new life is in store!

—Elaine Kennelly

Dear _____, I love you so much that I died for you. I desire to be in a relationship with you for the rest of your life. I promise to be your Shepherd, gently and lovingly leading you on the path I have chosen for you, and then, we can spend Eternity together.

Jesus

Day 2
Jesus Is Our Deliverance

*W*hen God created the universe, earth was perfect and Adam and Eve were perfect. Could He have created prewired "robot-people" who would love and obey Him always?

Yes ... but He didn't. He implanted the "seed of choice," as Max Lucado calls it. He created in us free-will. That is the option of choosing to love Him or not, choosing to obey Him or not, and choosing to live dependent on Him or not. You see, God is a gentleman and does not force Himself on anyone.

Adam and Eve chose disobedience and independence. They chose to believe Satan's lies and wanted to "be like God, knowing good and evil" (Genesis 3:5). But once they disobeyed God's command, they instantly knew evil. They understood evil. They felt evil for the very first time. You see, until that point, they were perfect; they knew only good and how good, good felt.

Here is our own personal dilemma: each of us must understand that we have no relationship with God unless we come face-to-face with the fact that we are sinful and need redemption.

Now for the very best part: God provided a way for our rescue.

Jesus left heaven for a while, and during that time, He took on human flesh and became a person. God named His Son

Immanuel, meaning "God with us." He did everything for us—in our place—living a perfect life and paying the price for Adam and Eve's poor choices and our poor choices.

Jesus suffered betrayal, torture, and even the savage death by hanging on a bloody cross until His final breath. That is a picture of what we should have had to bear. It's called the Father's cup of wrath, and Jesus drank every drop for you and me, because that is how great God's love is for us.

Jesus *wanted* to provide deliverance from our sin so that we could be in a loving relationship with Him. Jesus *wanted* to ransom us, redeem us, and provide a way for us to spend eternity in His presence. He *wanted* to save us from our sin, and that is why we can call Jesus our friend, our Savior, our deliverer.

Stop for a moment, and pray with me.

> Dear God, I realize that I am a sinner. I've been selfish, hurtful, dishonest, and full of lies. I am not proud of myself or the choices I am making. Forgive me and change me. I need your help. I need salvation, and I do want Heaven. I need *You*. Please come into my heart and life now. Amen.

God comes to you where you are, and your prayer is answered with a torrent of love that says, "Now, you are My child."

He loves you with an unfailing love, and forgiveness is yours no matter what you have done. There is no sin too great to be forgiven through the blood of Jesus Christ.

> For God presented Jesus as the sacrifice for sin. People are made right with God when they believe that Jesus sacrificed His life, shedding His blood. (Romans 3:25 NLT)

This is all yours, a gift to you from your Savior Jesus. Receive it in thankfulness and peace. You are forgiven!

Prayer

Oh, Father, I receive Your gift, and I believe that Jesus died for me, a sinner.

Thank You! In fact, words do not seem sufficient to really describe how grateful I am, and there is such peace in my heart. I feel like flying through the air, like telling the world, like laughing with a heart filled with so much joy!

I have never felt like this. I really am *Your child*. I belong to You. I am under Your care. I am clean and free from guilt, shame, anxiety, even loneliness. I belong to the family of God.

Keep me on Your path, Father. Show me what to do next and for all my tomorrows.

I love you. Amen.

You Can Say Yes to Jesus

There is no life so fallen,

That it cannot be forgiven.

There is no slate so dirty,

That it cannot be wiped clean.

There is no heart so darkly lit,

That Light could not pierce through it.

There is no mind so stubborn,

That God cannot intervene.

—Elaine Kennelly

Dear _____, I never force anyone to choose Me, love Me, or worship Me. Instead, I invite you to live in dependence on Me. There is nothing—no problem, no sin, and no heartache—that is too big for you and Me to handle together. That is My promise to you. My perfect love casts out fear.

Love, Jesus

Day 3
Jesus Is Our Sustenance

S ustenance—it's just a fancy word for food. It's our nourishment.

Jesus said,

> I am the bread of life. He who comes to Me will never go hungry, and he who believes in Me will never be thirsty. (John 6:35 NIV)

So how does that transfer into our daily life?

Jesus is not talking about popcorn or pizza. Instead, Jesus is talking about spiritual food—sustenance for your soul! How *do* we feed our souls? Has it ever occurred to you that you *need* to feed your soul?

Some of us have gone through the gate, found deliverance, and then starved ourselves to death. It happens all the time.

Remember the story of the farmer sowing seed? Where did the seed fall?

- Some fell on the well-worn path.

- Some fell on rocky places

- Some fell among the thorns and the weeds

- Some fell on good, fertile soil, where it produced a harvest.

Now *that* is a perfect word picture of us—you and me. Some of us let our deliverance decay, or we get so busy living our lives, we let it languish through neglect. Our busyness chokes out time for Jesus and His Word. We become spiritually starved, and our faith weakens.

Do you want to produce a fruitful harvest? Do you want your life to count for Jesus? Do you want to partake of spiritual sustenance and see spiritual growth? Yes! Yes! Yes!

Here's how:

- Don't allow your daily planner to become your priority.

- Take time each day to be alone in the presence of Jesus. I use my kitchen table, same chair every day. I savor the time in the presence of Jesus.

- Read your Bible, big chunks at a time. Read a devotional. Both can be downloaded onto your Smartphone or tablet for free (the Bible App, www.YouVersion.com). Take the time to do it today.

- Pray. Talk to God about your struggles, your longings, your emptiness. He already knows what's bothering you, so tell Him. Listening to you is important to God!

- Then be polite and listen to what God says to you. A reporter once asked Mother Teresa what she says to God when she prays. "I don't talk much. I mostly listen," was her reply.

You, too, can have the "mind of Christ" (1 Corinthians 2:16 NLT).

But it will take:

- Diligence and discipline on your part

- Time every day

- A real commitment to love God enough to learn how His thoughts can be your thoughts

Get together with other Bible-believing Christians. Oh, I can hear it coming now. "I don't like church." "Church is boring." "It's filled with hypocrites."

Going to church is *not about you!* It's about worshipping your heavenly Father, Your Savior, Jesus, and the Holy Spirit. It's about encouraging others around you. It's about giving back to God in sheer gratitude for deliverance and sustenance.

Feeding your faith is up to you. Remember, every person in the whole world has one thing exactly the same—time—24/7. Jesus can literally measure your love for Him by the amount of time you spend with Him each day.

So the choice is up to you. How much do you really love Him?

Prayer

Dear Jesus, it is my desire to produce a harvest of righteousness for You. I want to grow my faith every day, and for that to happen, I need You and the power of Your Holy Spirit.

Just like the flames of fire hovering over the first believers, send me Your Spirit to fill me with love, joy, patience, perseverance, and a willingness to share my faith with others.

I need You, the Word of God, and plenty of time for You. I love You, and I want to show You my love, my faith, my trust, and my dependence on You.

Lead me to a godly church that preaches the good news of Your book, the Bible.

Bless me to be a blessing to others everywhere.

In Jesus' precious name, I pray. Amen.

Growing My Faith

Jesus said if you had faith as tiny as a mustard seed,
You would be able to "move mountains." By God decreed!

So how come sometimes I can't even move myself?
My red-letter edition Bible just sits on the shelf.

It's too much to get up early after I've been out too late.
So Sunday comes and Sunday goes. God will have to wait.

But now I have a problem, it is serious and I'm ill.
The doctors call it cancer, with dreaded fear I am filled.

I need to read my Bible, spend time down on my knees!
"Oh, dear Lord, please heal me now," is my earnest plea.

God must shake His head, but He
still loves us, that's for sure.

He says, "Come to Me, believe in Me,
and trust Me for a cure."

"My child, I have blessed you—family,
house, and children three.

But none of these blessings seemed
to touch your heart for Me.

I wanted you to grow in faith and
have power for each day.

It didn't work with blessings, but
sickness paved the way.

So bring Me your prayers, your thanks, your problems, too.

Read My Word, trust in Me, and worship Me in truth."

—Elaine Kennelly

Dear_____, I am power for your life. Come and feed on Me. I will give you strength. I will uphold you with My righteous right arm. Come and spend time with Me, the Lamb of God, who loves you more than you will ever understand.

Jesus

Barbara and Elaine, The Original Something Sisters. (2010)

Day 4
Jesus Is Our Maintenance

*J*joke with my husband, Tom, by referring to myself as "high maintenance." And the older you get, the longer maintenance takes and the more expensive it becomes!

How do we get a picture of Jesus from the word "maintenance"? Think about the maintenance you do in your own yard, if you have one. It's work, isn't it?

> I am the true grapevine, and My Father is the gardener. He cuts off every branch of mine that doesn't produce fruit, and He prunes the branches that do bear fruit, so they will produce even more. (John 15:1–2 NLT)

God, the Father, owns the vineyard. He is the head gardener, and He is in charge. Jesus is the true grapevine. We are the branches, drawing our sustenance from Jesus.

> Remain in Me, and I will remain in you. For a branch cannot produce fruit if it is severed from the vine, and you cannot be fruitful unless you remain in Me. (John 15:4 NLT)

Maintenance is remaining in the relationship and keeping up the relationship so that after time, there will be results— tangible fruit. If you cut off every stem as a blossom appears on your pot of petunias, would you ever have flowers? No.

> If you remain in Me and My words remain in you, you may ask for anything you want, and it will be granted! (John 15:7 NLT)

You mean like the genie who pops out of the bottle to grant you three wishes? Hardly. If you stay attached to Jesus, you will bloom and continue to grow until you produce fruit. Keep reading.

> When you produce much fruit, you are My true disciples. This brings great glory to my Father. (John 15:8 NLT)

Now we've got the complete picture! Yes, God will give us what we ask for *if* we are His true disciples and *if* our requests bring glory to His Father. Why wouldn't God want to give us all these things?

Please note, there is no mention of time. We do have the tendency to want God's answers right away! His answer may be yes, but the timing is known only to God. Sometimes His answer is, "Dear _____, wait. I am teaching you so much throughout the waiting time." (Put your name in the space.)

> This is my commandment: Love each other in the same way I have loved you. There is no greater love than to lay down one's life for one's friends. (John 15:12 NLT)

It's interesting that Jesus equates obedience with love. If we love, we will obey, just as Jesus loved His Father so much that He was obedient, even to the point of dying on a cross. There can be no love relationship with God without obedience, not in heaven nor on earth.

Then out of obedience comes fruit.

> But the Holy Spirit produces this kind of fruit in our lives: Love, joy, peace, patience, kindness, goodness, faithfulness, gentleness and self-control. (Galatians 5:22–23a NLT)

After we bear fruit that will last, our relationship with Jesus becomes intimate.

Let that be our goal!

Prayer

Dearest Jesus, I see the garden, with Your Father tending it. He is gentle, but He prunes away every branch that does not bear fruit. Oh, Jesus, I want to bear fruit ... I really do.

Give me Your Holy Spirit power to follow Your instructions and Your guidance. Help me to listen to what You would like me to do. I don't need a big project, Jesus, but I want to be loving and helping and giving to others in my neighborhood, where I work, and at my church. It is my desire to love and help others.

Open my eyes to see Your path for my life and then may I be obedient. I so much want to hear You say, "Well done, good and faithful servant."

Holy Spirit empower me to serve others willingly, with a heart full of love for all people. Bless me to be a blessing to others this day.

Help me, Jesus, to be a person of service. In Your name I ask. Amen.

The Choice Is Ours

Jesus makes it very clear
In the 15th chapter of John,
Two actions we need to do,
A response we must act upon.

He gives a command—remain in Him,
To stay, dwell, and reside.
A choice with an assurance for all,
He promises in us to abide.

"Remain in Me and I in you."
The choice is ours to make.
Our love for Him, our trust,
Plus obedience are all at stake.

We have to choose where it is
We want to inhabit and to live.
Is it back to sin and self, or
To Jesus to bear fruit and give?

"*I am the vine, and as the branch,*
You take root in Me.
Then I provide all that you need
To live life fruitfully."

By fruit, I mean, you will be able,
Others, to love and forgive,
To tithe, to trust, to tell the world
How in Me you choose to live.

Apart from Me, your life is
Shallow, aimless, and bare.
Living in Me, you'll have My joy,
My peace, and My eternal care."
—*Elaine Kennelly*

Dear _____, stay on your life path with Me, and I will remain in you, but you must remain dependent on Me. I will always keep My part of our relationship. I will never leave you or forsake you. Instead, I will fill you with My love so that you will bear fruit, such as joy, peace, kindness, and self-control. Trust Me.

Jesus

Day 5
Jesus Is Our Inheritance

*a*n inheritance is a future gift.

Sometimes an earthly inheritance might put a smile on our faces, and then again, sometimes we might not be too happy about getting Aunt Erma's spoon collection—one from each state in America.

But I have great news for you. Listen to what the Bible has to say about our inheritance.

> All praise to God, the Father of our Lord Jesus Christ. It is by His great mercy that we have been born again, because God raised Jesus Christ from the dead. Now we live with great expectation, and we have a priceless inheritance—an inheritance that is kept in Heaven for you, pure and undefiled, beyond the reach of change and decay. (1 Peter 1:3–4 NLT)

On that first Easter morning, when God raised His Son from the grip of death, sin, and Satan, we received an eternal inheritance that is indeed priceless. It is positive proof of our salvation—eternity in heaven.

Amazing grace gives eternal life! Jesus is our inheritance. We will live forever with Him.

> And through your faith, God is protecting you by His Power until you receive this salvation, which is ready to be revealed on the last day for all to see. So be truly glad. There is wonderful joy ahead, even though

> you have to endure many trials for a little while. (1 Peter 1:5–6 NLT)

Ahhh, there is good news/bad news going on here: God is protecting us by His power—that's good. We will have to endure many trials while living here on earth—that's not so good.

But as delivered believers, we need to understand that trials will come. They will be a part of our life here on earth now. Be prepared.

In Psalm 46:10, it says, "Be still and know that I am God." In other translations, these phrases are used instead of "Be still": "Stop fighting" (GNT), "Let go of your concerns" (GWT), and my favorite, "Cease striving and know that I am God" (NASB).

Memorize this important Scripture: "I can do everything through Him (Christ) who gives me strength" (Philippians 4:13 NIV).

Here's something else you need to know about your inheritance.

> Whatever you do, work at it with all your heart, as working for the Lord, not for men, since you know that you will receive an inheritance from the Lord as a reward. It is the Lord Christ you are serving. (Colossians 3:23–24 NIV)

Wow! Wouldn't America change overnight if all Christians worked that way at their jobs!

Ephesians 1:18 (NLT) continues to encourage us now.

> I pray that your hearts will be flooded with light so that you can understand the confident hope He has given to those He called—His holy people who are His rich and glorious inheritance.

And one of my all-time favorites.

Are not all angels ministering spirits sent to serve those who will inherit salvation? (Hebrews 1:14 NIV)

I thank God every day for sending His angels to be with me, protecting me, watching over me. (Have you ever seen me drive?)

Just imagine—God, in His great love, not only gave His Son to us freely but sends His personal angels to minister to us now.

Without a doubt, Jesus is our inheritance now, and it is secured through the cross and resurrection for all eternity.

Prayer

Precious Jesus, my Lord, my Master, I am overwhelmed with joy at the thought of an inheritance from You! Spending eternity in Your presence provides a picture of peace for me. When I get frustrated or worried, help me to remember my eternal gift from You. Send the Holy Spirit to me, dear Jesus, so that I will become stronger in my faith and trust.

Thank you for sending angels to protect me and my loved ones. I give up my spouse, my parents, my children, and my grandchildren into your hands, entrusting them to you. Keep them safe, protect them from the evil in the world, and give them your Holy Spirit.

I give my deepest thanks and my sweetest praise to you, Jesus, for providing amazing grace and eternal life. Eternity will not be long enough to give You adequate worship, honor, glory, and praise. Heaven will be such joy!

I love you so much, Jesus. Amen.

I'm But a Stranger Here

I'm but a stranger here, Heav'n is my home;

Earth is a desert drear, Heav'n is my home.

Danger and sorrow stand round me on every hand;

Heaven is my fatherland, Heav'n is my home.

Therefore I murmur not, Heav'n is my home;

What e'er my earthly lot, Heav'n is my home;

And I shall surely stand there at my Lord's right hand.

Heav'n is my fatherland, Heav'n is my home.

—Thomas R. Taylor,1807–1835,Lutheran Worship Hymnal

Dear _____, yes, you may live in great expectation, because I have a priceless inheritance waiting for *you*, my Child. It's called heaven! Through your faith, I am protecting you, even through pain and troubles. Never lose your hope in Me! I am trustworthy, because nothing will ever separate you from My love.

Jesus

Day 6
A Prayer and an Answer

*J*love the book of Psalms! I love the emotions. Every chapter has its ups and downs, except for Psalm 88. When you are depressed or grieving, Psalm 88 will not cheer you up, but you will feel affirmed by the knowledge that someone else once felt as miserable as you. I found that to be comforting.

The only time I ever heard a pastor or teacher mention Psalm 88, was in Jerusalem, when Tom and I were touring the Holy Land. The guide thought that the Thursday night of Jesus' arrest, as He was imprisoned, He was quite possibly reciting Psalm 88.

But I have good news for you today. This message does not go anywhere near Psalm 88!

We are in my favorite book, and I want to share with you a message that has changed the way I go to sleep at night and how I wake up in the morning.

> Let the morning bring me word of your unfailing love, for I have put my trust in you. Show me the way I should go, for to you I entrust my life. (Psalm 143:8 NLT)

For many years, I had trouble believing God really loved me. I started searching out Bible verses that would point to God's love, and there were so many. God is overly generous in His continual assurance of His love for us. I started using

Psalm 143:8 as a prayer every night. They are the last words I think of before I fall asleep.

I memorized that verse, and that was not easy for me. Here is what I do to memorize Bible verses:

- I print the verse on a 3 x 5 card. Might need a 4 x 6 inch card now that my eyesight is getting aged.

- Put the verse on at least four cards. Use one as a bookmark in your daily devotional book.

- Put one on the refrigerator.

- One goes on the mirror in the bathroom.

- One goes in the car, plastered on the dashboard.

Something Sisters, put them wherever you will read them! Over and over again, let the words of our heavenly Father penetrate your heart, mind, and memory. Ask God to help you memorize, and He will. Pretty soon, the verse is yours, bonded in your heart as well as in your mind.

Then a very wonderful coincidence—"God-incidence" as I like to call it—happened. God led me to another verse in the book of Psalms.

> I will instruct you and teach you in the way you should go; I will counsel you with my loving eye on you. (Psalm 32:8 NLT)

The "I" here is God: Father, Papa, Creator. He gave me His direct answer from Scripture that complements my prayer in Psalm 143:8 (NLT). Let's put the two verses together.

> My prayer: Let the morning bring me word of your unfailing love, for I have put my trust in you. *Show me the way I should go,* for to you I entrust my life.

God's answer: I will instruct you and teach you *in the way you should go*. I will counsel you with My loving eye on you.

My prayer—God's beautiful answer. Let it control the way you think as you gently fall asleep, and may it be on your lips or in your mind the first thing every morning.

It will change your attitude as you start your day. I promise!

Prayer

Heavenly Father, thank You for giving us the Bible, in which You, the Creator, share Yourself generously with us, Your creation. You are forever declaring Your gracious and unfailing love to us. Without a doubt in my heart, I know You love me. Thank you, dear Papa!

As I read your words and pray Your prayers, I realize You love me, You have always loved me, and You will love me forever, through all eternity. I am humbled that You, the God of the universe, love me, a sinner, and I rejoice in my salvation in Christ.

Show me each day, O Lord, the path You want me to take. Teach me in the way I should go. I willingly follow You, because each day with You is an adventure! Increase my trust and my faith as I walk with You each day.

I love You, Papa, and I am trusting that You will help me to memorize Your Holy Word.

Your loving daughter, _____. Amen.

A Prayer and an Answer

Sometimes I pray to God
and His answer is to … wait.
I don't like to hear that.
I like my answers straight
To the point. Is it yes, or is it no?
I want my answer right away.
Make up your mind today!

Sometimes I pray to God
And His answer is … no.
I don't like to hear that,
Because I want to keep control.
Will you listen up … Oh, God?
Answer "just this once" with a yes,
'Cause I really do deserve to be blessed!

Sometimes I pray to God.

There is silence all around.

Not a peep. Not a stir.

Nothing's going heavenward

My words are still on earth.

I will have to say them louder,

For they're of infinite worth!

Ahhh! I've found that when I pray

To God—the verses in His Word,

My prayers are always perfect,

And they are always heard.

The book of Psalms has every prayer

I need to send God's way. And He

Always has THE answer—sent without delay!

—Elaine Kennelly

Dear _____, I love it when you spend time in My book. It was written for all people, but especially for you, my daughter, whom I treasure with all My heart. I will "show you the way to go" each day. So rely on Me, and stop worrying about what might happen. I am in control. Nothing happens to you that I do not allow.

Love, Jesus

Day 7
Changing My Thought Patterns

*M*y brain never seems to quit. It churns and swirls. It plays words and scenes over and over and over again. Sometimes my thoughts are my own worst enemy.

I talk to myself and say things like, "You blew it again. Why didn't you say this?" Or, "Why did you say that?" "It was my fault." "Where did I fail?" "I did such a stupid thing."

My travel agent has me on a permanent list for trips ... the ones called guilt. But it's really not funny, is it?

In my head, I know guilt is not God's plan for me or for you, my precious friends. Guilt is not part of God's vocabulary. In fact, it is the exact opposite.

> For God did not send his Son into the world to condemn the world, but to save the world through Him. Whoever believes in Him is not condemned. (John 3:17–18a NIV)

> Therefore, there is now no condemnation for those who are in Christ Jesus. (Romans 8:1 NIV)

There is a place for guilt in our lives, as God prompts us to confess our sin and receive His gracious gift of grace. But guilt that continues to creep into your conscience, over and over, blaming you, accusing you, finding fault with you is just plain wrong.

Consistent guilt is a tool of Satan, and some of us, especially mothers, have an Achilles heel Satan and all of his demons know quite well: "Just say to her, you failed again."

> But those who live in accordance with the Spirit [of God] have their minds set on what the Spirit desires. The mind of sinful man is death, but the mind controlled by the Spirit is life and peace. (Romans 8:5b–6 NIV)

> But letting the Spirit control your mind leads to life and peace. (Romans 8:6a NLT)

Isn't that what all of us crave—life and peace? Of course it is! But how do we get there?

We get there by fully understanding we are totally right with God. We are clothed in the satisfying salvation of Jesus Christ. The price for our sin has been paid in full. When we pray to God, He sees us as His holy perfect children, wrapped in redemption.

- Trust Jesus! Don't analyze. Don't agonize. Take Jesus and His gift of salvation into your heart, forever. Believe it. Don't doubt it. Rejoice in it. Thank God for it. Preach the gospel to yourself every day.

- Ask the Holy Spirit to take charge of your life, starting *now.* The Bible says that *we must let* our minds be controlled by the Holy Spirit. Give up your spiritual driver's license! Let the Holy Spirit *drive,* and you will have life and peace.

- Give up the old blockages that clog your cognitive thinking. They build up like plaque in your veins, choking out life, little by little, until you become hard and bitter. *Let go of the past,* and rid your mind of repetitive, negative thoughts.

  Don't copy the behavior and customs of this world, but let God transform you into a new person by changing the way you think. Then you will learn to know God's will for you, which is good and pleasing and perfect. (Romans 12:2 NLT)

Something Sisters, you have to make up your mind and then do it.

Prayer

My precious Papa, I come to you today knowing full well that I have some old, stubborn blockages that I allow to remain in the darkest crevices of my mind. Satan wants me to keep them there, and, quite honestly, I want to keep them there on some days. Then I can feel sorry for myself and continue to wallow in the hurt, injustice, sorrow, and suffering of it all. I know that my self-guilt is fed by my self-pride.

Papa, in the name of Jesus, forgive my stubbornness. It's as though I dare to defy You. I almost want to be miserable. No, I really don't want to be miserable. I don't want to sink into bitterness. Bitterness is ugly, and I want to be beautiful for You. Bitterness is sad, and I want to sing with the joy of the Lord in my heart.

Bitterness is dangerous, and I want to be safe. My loving heart will eventually erode, and I will end up in the twilight of my life with a heart of stone—if I follow the path of stubbornness.

Allow me, Father, to change the way I think. Lead me to know Your will, which is good and pleasing and perfect. Help me, Jesus, through the power of Your Spirit. Amen.

God Is with Me—I'm Loved

You tested me, Lord, in my darkest of days;

I could only weep, and tears were my "praise."

For years all I wanted was to be left alone.

From me came silence; my heart became stone.

I was rebellious. So stubborn.

You loved.

Had You been in charge, I would've healed swift and sweet;

But in Your great love, You allowed anguished defeat.

Your gracious free will—Satan makes it sound so good.

I listened to him, and his lies became food.

I was hungry. So starved.

You loved.

Tho' years went by, You continued to bless.

I did not receive You; nor did I want to confess.

So what came about in the depths of my heart?

I missed Your sweet solace; my life fell apart.

I was lost. So alone.

You loved.

In hindsight, now I see ever so clearly

That all along, You loved me ever so dearly.

Your Spirit was close to me, right at my side;

My stubbornness forgiven when Jesus Christ died.

I am whole. I am healed.

You loved.

How does one live with a safe second chance?

A huge "do over"—another try at "the dance"?

It's doable, I promise. Just only believe.

Open wide your heart, and Christ Jesus receive.

I'm thankful. I'm grateful.

I'm loved!

—Elaine Kennelly

Dear _____, I will untangle all the webs of misguided thinking in your mind, and I will put a stop to all your repetitive negative thoughts. But you must give them to Me, once and for all. Do not snatch them back! I am God, in charge of everything! I can change you—if you want to be changed.

Jesus

Elaine and Marnie, while on a trip to Hawaii. (2006)

Day 8
The Heavens Declare
the Glory of God

*H*aleakala is Hawaiian for "house of the sun." It was anything but "sunshine hot" as we ascended to the top of the upper slopes of Haleakala on the island of Maui. Marnie, one of my closest and dearest Something Sisters, her husband, David, plus Tom and I were in the car.

It was 4:00 a.m., pitch dark, and very quiet. No one was ahead of our car, or behind. We were driving slowly upward, always upward, with the intent to watch the sun rise over this volcanic crater.

And it was cold. We bundled up with whatever we could find in our suitcases to keep warm. (When packing for Hawaii, somehow, you don't think long underwear!)

Tom suddenly stopped the car and motioned for all of us to get out and look up. What I saw and experienced will forever be one of the most spectacular memories of my life on earth.

The sky exploded with brilliant light! Sparkle and brilliance I had never experienced were everywhere. In the intense darkness, I marveled at the millions of dazzling stars, gleaming and flashing more intensely than I had ever seen. I was reminded,

> The Heavens proclaim the glory of God. The skies display His craftsmanship. Day after day they continue to speak; night after night they make Him known. They speak without a sound or word; their voice is

never heard. Yet their message has gone throughout the earth, and their words to all the world. (Psalm 19:1–4 NLT)

He counts the stars and calls them all by name. How great is our Lord! His power is absolute! His understanding is beyond comprehension! (Psalm 147:4–5 NLT)

The only word that comes to my mind when I try to comprehend the glory of the Lord is "more." God is always more than we can understand … more than we can know, grasp, assimilate, fathom, or appreciate.

God is God!

We are to worship our magnificent God, who created everything we see and everything we don't see. He is worthy of our worship, not just on Sunday, but every day of the week.

Something Sisters, if you want your inner spirit to soar, and if you want joy in your daily routine, praise and worship are for you. You can say your worship, sing your worship, or pray your worship to the great God of the universe.

Oh, how great are God's riches and wisdom and knowledge! How impossible it is for us to understand His decisions and His ways! … For everything comes from Him and exists by His power and is intended for His glory. All glory to Him forever! Amen. (Romans 11:33–34, 36 NLT)

Prayer

Oh, magnificent Lord, how awesome You are! I fall on my knees in worship and adoration of You and Your holy splendor. You are worthy of my praise and the praise of every human ever born. You and Your love for me is more than I can ever take in ... more than I can embrace. How marvelous You are and how graciously You give us all things.

You are the only God of the universe, King of Kings and Lord of Lords! I wish there were special words created just to praise You, to glorify Your holy name, to thank You for Your almighty goodness.

The universe and everything in it has been created by You, maintained and sustained throughout generations by Your power and might, and for that I am extremely thankful and humbled by Your sweet love for me.

You are most worthy of my praise!

In the powerful name of Jesus, I pray. Amen.

If Stars Could Speak

Come with me, and let's pretend we live within the sky.

For just one night, we'll leave the earth, nature to defy.

Come, let's pretend we are soaring high above the earth,

And night has come; as stars, we've been rebirthed.

The first star that I meet says, "Hey, what is your name?"

I quickly say, "I don't have one," and bow my head in shame.

"You don't have a name? Why that's not how it is done.
The Father comes each night and names us, one by one.

Hurry, be a shooting star, and go straight to His throne.
He'll give you a name, one that's all your very own."

So I became a brilliant shooting star and went so very fast.
Across the heavens I zoomed! Wow! This is a blast!

And then a hand so gently came and touched my pointy end.
"You are new tonight, dear star, what is your name, my friend?"

With head bowed low, I said so soft, "Dear God, I need a name."
"Well," He said with authority, "I have one for you to claim!

I will name you Marvelous and Brilliance. As you shine,
You will declare My glory and My presence you'll define.

You'll go straight to earth to a place called Bethlehem,
And you will show the world the gift that I have sent.

The gift to all is My begotten Son—the world He will redeem.
And with your Marvelous Brilliance, this message you will beam."

—Elaine Kennelly

Dear _____, I love to receive your worship and praise. You have been touched by My beauty, and you appreciate the awesome universe I created. Keep your eyes open to see Me in every part of nature, for I am there. You will find Me, and I will bless you, My dear daughter.

Love, Jesus

Day 9
Chosen by God for Greatness

*M*oses. Just the sound of his name is distinguished. Then, of course, I think of Charlton Heston, the Moses in my memory. Tall, handsome, rugged, challenging, skin touched by the sun; why he was the epitome of every leader chosen by God to do a great deed.

Ahhh ... the "Hollywood Harbinger," the "Herald of Headlines" ... Moses is God's messenger. Extra! Extra! Read all about it!

> God speaks, "The Israelite cry for help has come to me, and I've seen for myself how cruelly they're being treated by the Egyptians. It's time for you to go back: I am sending you to Pharaoh to bring my people, the People of Israel, out of Egypt." (Exodus 3:9 The Message)

> Moses answered God *(in a whiny voice)*, "But why me? What makes you think that I could ever go to Pharaoh and lead the children of Israel out of Egypt?" (Exodus 3:10 The Message; parenthetical comments mine.)

But why me? That could not possibly be in the script! Moses wouldn't say, "But ... why me?" In the King James version, Moses says, "Who am I, that I should go unto Pharaoh?" It's like, "God, you have got to be kidding. You don't really mean me, do you?"

Moses ... reduced to reality ... dazed by doubt ... instantly incredulous. Now, there is someone I can identify with.

We could go through the entire Bible and find example after example of people chosen by God to do a great deed who were frightened, doubtful, fearful men and women. Just like Moses.

Jacob, out of fear, fled to his uncle Laban's house ... for twenty years.

Over and over again, God said to Joshua, "Be strong and courageous. Do not be terrified" (Joshua 1:9 NIV).

Gideon said, "*Me,* my master? How and with what could I ever save Israel? Look at me. My clan's the weakest ... and I'm the runt of the litter" (Judges 6:15 The Message, Also spoken in a whiny voice).

Ruth loses every means of earning a living. Her husband and two sons die. She is destitute and homeless. She runs away.

Saul, chosen to be King Saul, hid in the baggage room (1 Samuel 10:22).

David confesses in Psalm 38:7–8 (in another whiny voice), "My back is filled with searing pain; there is no health in my body. I am feeble and utterly crushed; I groan in anguish of heart."

Esther has to have sex with a stranger, someone who could have her head chopped off at any moment.

Peter denounces his association with Jesus. All of the closest friends of Jesus desert him in the garden of Gethsemane. Thomas doubts Jesus' appearance after His resurrection.

Paul of Tarsus, says, "When we came into Macedonia ... we had conflicts on the outside, fears within" (2 Corinthians 7:5 NIV).

Now, what about you? Dear Something Sisters, we have all been chosen by God for greatness and equipped by God to accomplish His desires.

> For God is working in you, giving you the desire and the power to do what pleases Him. (Philippians 2:13 NLT)

> You can make many plans, but the LORD's purpose will prevail." (Proverbs 19:21 NIV)

But then in weakness I say to God, "I love *my* agenda, *my* plan, and I like all *my* ducks in a row. *I want* the control. *I want* to be the decision maker."

Then God says, "Elaine, enjoy each day with Me as I lead you down the pathway that *I* have created for *you*. Each Something Sister has her own path, designed by Me, to use her God-given gifts and talents. Urge your Something Sisters to trust Me, to be in relationship with Me, to pray for guidance on the path, and to thank Me in all circumstances. Stay close to Me as I lead."

That is what God led me to write in my journal on June 16, 2012.

Prayer

Heavenly Father, I can so relate to everyone's response to your calling. I, too, feel under-equipped and overly afraid that you should expect me to write a book and put a website together. I'm in the last quadrant of my life! I don't have the computer skills! Who would listen to me? I'm just a nobody, and I have never written a book, (as I speak in a whiny voice.)

He answers my prayer. "Be still, My child, and listen to Me: I have called you, and I will equip you. I will give you

My thoughts and My words. You are My servant. I am the author and giver of all you will need. Trust Me, and lean on Me as we go down your pathway. What an adventure! Your loving Papa."

God's Path for You

We all have a path called an Adventure with God.

God leads you and guides you. It's His path you trod.

He takes you to places you would never choose.

He wants you to trust; your fears all to lose.

Sometimes the path goes on forever, it seems;

A difficult path filled with emotional extremes.

Then God brings a day. It's such a terrible waste.

It's dull, boring, and empty, no flavor to taste.

Surprise! He takes you through a flowery field.

There's lots of fun; the joy is never concealed.

The secret to enjoying this adventure with Him?

Go out of your comfort zone. Go out on a limb!

Have faith in your path and Your Father, who leads.

Have trust in His goodness. He'll supply all your needs.

—Elaine Kennelly

I have a purpose for your life, dear _____. Just give Me yourself, and I will supply you with all you need to accomplish all that I desire. But you must trust Me first. Is it hard to trust Me? Then you do not realize how much I love you. Please be reassured that I love you with a divine love that never fails.

Jesus

The Beach Beauties, all Concordia University Chicago alumni, gathering at Orange Beach, Alabama. (2010)

Day 10
God Is Shining on Me

*J*n the Old Testament, God gives a wonderful blessing! However, it's found in an odd place in Scripture. You have to be on a treasure hunt to find it.

Dust off the book of Numbers. You might even have to look in the contents to find where it is. Tell me truthfully: have you *ever* read the entire book all at one time without falling asleep somewhere between chapter 1 and chapter 2?

If there is a Something Sister out there who loves math, enjoys numbers, adores algebra, and connects with calculus—praise the Lord! Or as they would say in the South, "Bless your heart." Oh, I have a Something Sister, Angie, who teaches math to middle-schoolers! Hooray for her!

Now here is the "pearl" we find on our treasure hunt. I'm going to extract it from the King James Version, because I think it will bring back fond memories for many of us.

The LORD bless Thee and keep thee.

The LORD make His face shine upon thee,

and be gracious unto thee.

The LORD lift up His countenance upon thee,

and give thee peace. (Numbers 6:24)

One of my favorite childhood memories is hearing these words from my pastor at the end of every church service.

It was comforting. I felt so close to God. It was as though I could feel the shine from God's face on my face.

Here's what happened a few years ago. God led me to understand that His Words, the words we call Scripture, belong to each one of us personally. He takes great delight when we take the words and make them our own.

I call it personalizing Scripture. Take a verse and make it your very own, putting your name right at the beginning, middle, or end. Or take the "you" and make it "me."

I have taken Numbers 6:24 and made it my personal blessing.

The LORD bless me and keep me;

The LORD make His face shine upon me and be

gracious to me;

The LORD lift up His countenance (His favor) upon me and give me peace.

I urge you to say this prayer often, especially as you invite God into your day. You could say this as you wake up in the morning, even before you get out of bed.

Dear friends, I feel with all my heart that God wants us to take His words and make them come alive inside of us, make them personal, make them ours, committing them to our memories and our lives.

Here are some more of my favorites.

> For I am the LORD, your God, who takes hold of your right hand and says to you, "Do not fear. I will help you. Do not be afraid, O little _____." (Isaiah 41:13–14 NIV)

> My grace is sufficient for you, _____, for My power is made perfect in your weakness. (2 Corinthians 12:9 NIV)

Let your face shine on your servant, _____;
Save me in your unfailing love. (Psalm 31:16 NIV)

My dear friends, take God's Word and make it yours. Put your name in the blanks. Oh, go ahead ... do it now!

Prayer

Dear Father, I am always amazed at how You want to be in a personal relationship with me. You consider me to be important to You, and You want to spend time with me. Thank You for Your unfailing love, mercy, and grace, Your provision and Your passion toward Your children, those who believe in You and trust in You.

Thank You for your very own words, written down centuries ago, so that I might come to know You better and love You more. Your Word is Truth, and I am thrilled to make it my own.

Help me through the power of the Holy Spirit to desire your words more than anything in my life. Help me to share Your word with others, so all may come to the knowledge of the truth—Jesus Christ—and believe in Him.

I pray in the power of Jesus Himself. Amen.

God's Beauty Treatment

As I come every morning to meet with my Lord,

I sit at my kitchen table, my love for Him adored.

Happily I come, the first hour of each new day,

Knowing I will be refreshed in Jesus 'long the way.

Father taught me to take His words as my very own,

To claim them to memory or write them in a poem.

His words are important; they are truth on every page;

We must put them in our heart, no matter what our age.

He has a special blessing He gives me every day.

It's my Beauty Treatment, according to God's way.

I put my face directly up to God, who is my Lord,

Cup my hands around my face, these words I do outpour.

"The Lord bless me and keep me, in Your way, so divine.

Shine Your heavenly Light from Your face down to mine.

Please be gracious to my face, take those wrinkles all away.

Shine Your favor on my life. Now hurry! Don't delay!"

—Elaine Kennelly

Dear _____, I love it when you start your morning with Me. I created you to be in close contact with Me and My Father and the My Spirit. Remember, it's called relationship, and every relationship has conversations. Talk to Me throughout the day, and I will answer. In the quiet moments of the day, please listen.

Jesus

Day 11
When God Writes You a Letter

ear Something Sisters,

Today, I, God, am going to speak to you personally. I'm giving Elaine the day off.

I wrote the Bible, not as a tribute to Me, which it actually is, but for My creation, My creatures called "people." Human beings were created just a little lower than angelic beings. But you know that, don't you?

My intention was for people to connect with Me in a beautiful relationship of trust, love, and obedience—like family—like child to parent and parent to child.

The outcome? I knew even before I started creating that free-will would change everything. But I wanted to do it. Otherwise, you'd all be robots.

But *I am God.* I always act on your behalf. I love you so much, I put another plan in place, and I call it *grace.* It stands for God *r*edeems *a*ll *c*reatures *e*verywhere.

Writing the Bible wasn't difficult, you know. I give My thoughts to people all the time. They are a gift of the Holy Spirit.

In fact, here is something quite memorable. My very first attempt was done on a grand scale. I created a "finger" on My hand that, when placed on a granite tablet from Mount Sinai, cut the Ten Commandments right into the rock, word for word. (And you think Galaxy tablets are new!)

The Holy Bible is:

- My plan of salvation offered to everyone

- My promises, which are always kept

- My personal relationship builder

- My encouragement to human beings

- My pointed finger of conviction

- My training manual in how to live on earth with other flawed beings

- My Ten Commandments

- My lessons in holiness

- My gift of Holy Spirit gifts

- My character revealed

- My portion of history, which I have chosen to share with you

- My picture of heaven

- My plan for the end of this creation and beginning of a new heaven and a new earth

My Words are total truth, and *this is important*. They are truth, written by people, but with My Holy Spirit to guide them. When you read the Bible, you can rest assured and have total confidence that I am talking to *you.*

Of course, it is a "condensed version." Because you cannot fully comprehend Me, I had to put words on paper, so you would be able to understand and believe. I am even bigger and better and beyond the Bible. I am *more* than you can understand.

Truthfully, I have chosen not to reveal everything about Myself, but I choose to give you My truth, assurances, and promises regarding your life.

Plus I leave room for trust and hope and obedience. After all, isn't that what a relationship is all about?

I want to be your God, and I want you to be My child. I want all to be saved and to come to the knowledge of the truth.

There! That's it! That is exactly what the Bible is—the knowledge of the truth. Please read it, and believe it. Call on My name, and you will be saved.

Eternal Love,

Your Father, your Savior, and your Holy Spirit

P.S. I leave a lot of good stuff out, especially about the future and heaven, and what you will do for eternity. You're going to *love* it!

Prayer

Oh, God, how I desire Your friendship. I want to be in relationship with You.

Thank You for talking to me about Yourself. I have so much access to You, and yet I don't take advantage of it all. Forgive my negligence and my pride in thinking that I can live independently of You. That is impossible, for You are forgiveness, love, mercy, and grace, and I cannot live without You, Lord.

Help me to read the Word, and help me to put Scripture on my phone, my tablet, my computer, even my MP3 player, Kindle, or Nook. I want to make a commitment to read from my Bible every day—not out of obligation but out of love for You. Help me through the power of the Holy Spirit to accomplish this.

Thank You for your unfailing love! Thank You for caring for me as Your beloved child, for You, dear Jesus, are my beloved friend.

I love You. Amen.

God Is Always More

God and His vastness is more than I can see,

More than you or I could ever hope to be.

Why, if I could, for just a day or two,

Comprehend His being ...

No! That—I could never do.

The magnitude of God is more than I can feel

More than you and I could ever hope to reveal.

Why, if I could, for just a day or two,

Know His magnitude ...

No! That—I could never do.

Unfathomable is He; more than I can take in is He.

He's more than you or I could ever hope to be.

Why, if I could, for just a day or two,

Understand His mind ...

No! That—I could never do.

Something Sisters

You see, if I could perhaps understand or comprehend

The mind of God, His being, without beginning or end,

Then ... I would *be* God, and

That—I could never do.

How tragic to make God so small

that we should understand His ways.

How sad to have a God

Who is puny, insufficient, and ceases to amaze.

How cruel to pretend that God is only

As big as my mind can understand.

How happy I am that my God has the

Whole of creation at His command!

Yes, my God is bigger and grander

and deeper and higher than all.

And my mind is puny and shallow

And petty and small.

Praise God for His magnitude, His vastness

We cannot comprehend!

Praise God, whom we shall worship and adore

And trust forever without end!

—Elaine Kennelly

Dear _____, I am the Alpha and Omega, the beginning and the end. My understanding has no limit. I am everywhere. I know everything, and I hold all the power of the universe in My hand. I am trustworthy. Look beyond your momentary problems and see Me, the One in whom you can trust.

Jesus

Day 12
Anoint Me with the Oil of Joy

*I*n our culture today, happiness and joy are pretty much synonymous. In fact, if you go to *www.dictionary. com,* that is what you will see. I wish I could say it was that easy and uncomplicated.

I can't, and it's not.

The good news: joy is the complete understanding that there is nothing—I mean absolutely nothing—that can separate you from the love of God.

> And I am convinced that nothing can ever separate us from God's love. Neither death, nor life, neither angels, nor demons, neither our fears for today nor our worries about tomorrow not even the powers of hell can separate us from God's love. No power in the sky above or in the earth below—indeed, nothing in all creation will ever be able to separate us from the love of God that is revealed in Christ Jesus our Lord. (Romans 8:38–39 NLT)

My dear Something Sisters, do you really believe that? What if you were raped or sexually abused as a child or teenager? Does God still love you?

What if your child died? Or you miscarried many times and were never able to have a child? Or your teenage children are making very dangerous choices? Does God still love you?

What if your beautiful grandchild has cancer or was killed by a drunk driver? Or you, yourself, have just months to live? Or your precious husband died prematurely? Or maybe he left you for a younger woman? Or you never had a husband? What if your Something Sister just passed away, and you are crying as you read this?

What if? What if? What if?

The list is endless, because we live in a broken world. There will always be heartaches, sickness, death, sin, hardships, and evil as we live day by day on this fallen planet called earth.

In order for you to be anointed with the oil of joy, you must know and believe beyond a shadow of a doubt that nothing can get between you and God's love. Nothing!

That's the good news. The bad news is that I think you will never experience spectacular and sensational joy until you can willingly surrender *everything* to the God in charge of this fallen and broken world.

Surrender ... yield ... let go ... and say,

> You, Papa, may have Your way with my life. You may have my marriage, my children and grandchildren, my family, my job, my finances, my home, my health, my safety, my retirement, even my mind. I let go of it all. It's *all* Yours.

Then, and only then, dear Something Sisters, will you find true and lasting joy.

In the book of Nehemiah, the Jewish people who listened to God and returned to Israel from Babylon had to know beyond a doubt that God loved them. They had to believe that nothing—not hatred, lies, fatigue, or even enemy attack—could separate them from God's deep love and care for them.

They persevered, they trusted, they surrendered their fear, their families, and their future to Jahweh, Jehovah, our great God.

At the end of their monumental task, their governor, Nehemiah, reassures them with these words: "The joy of the Lord is your strength" (Nehemiah 8:10b NIV).

One of my favorite verses comes from Psalm 45:7, out of the old NIV version: "Therefore God, your God, has set you above your companions by anointing you with the oil of joy."

My mental picture of God's love, the oil of joy, is flowing down upon me, not only on the outside, but even more specially, on the inside, down into the depths of my soul. At the same time, I am lifting my hands in worship and surrendering all that is meaningful to me to my heavenly Father.

Oh, Lord, anoint us today with the oil of joy!

Prayer

Everlasting Father, my heart is so filled with Your love, Your real love, that is demonstrated every day I am alive! Even though there has been sorrow and sadness in my life, I do know, understand, and accept Your perfect love for me.

Just the thought of Jesus giving His life as a ransom for me and the thought of You, Father, raising Him from the dead is proof positive of Your generous gift of love.

I surrender all to You, Sovereign Lord, all that I have and all that I am. I yield to Your will for my life, knowing Your love surrounds me.

Anoint me with the oil of joy today, and may it be evident in my life. Bless me to be a blessing to others!

In Jesus' loving name I pray. Amen.

Nothing Is Wasted

Nothing is wasted, when you walk close to Me!

Not trials, they bring trust.

Not fear, it grows faith.

Not sickness, healing provides patience.

Not anger, it releases, gives rest.

Not problems, they force prayer.

Not temptation, it reaps restraint.

Not pride, it can be pruned.

Not judgment, humility is honed.

Not suffering, for when suffering is surrendered,

Joy brings Peace to the Soul.

—Elaine Kennelly

Dear _____, you are my special delight, because you delight yourself in Me! You talk with Me and laugh with Me. So few of My daughters come to Me for joy. But real joy flows from Me. Real joy can be in your life, even when circumstances seem difficult. My joy will give you strength.

Love, Jesus

*Elaine and Rosie, roommates at Concordia Teachers
College, River Forest, Illinois - previous name of
Concordia University Chicago. (2010)*

Day 13
For the Joy Set before Him

*D*r. David Jeremiah, pastor and founder of Turning Point Ministries, states that "Joy is a by-product, not a goal. Joy is the result of another action, which we identified as surrender—complete surrender to God."

Here is where we have to grow up, my dear Something Sisters, especially if you have been a believer for a long time. We need to become mature in our surrender and submission to God.

Let's take a look at the example Jesus gave to us.

Let us keep our eyes fixed on Jesus, on whom our faith depends from beginning to end. He did not give up because of the cross! On the contrary, because of the joy that was waiting for Him, He thought nothing of the disgrace of dying on the cross, and He is now seated at the right side of God's throne. (Hebrews 12:2 GNT)

I chose this particular version for these words, "Because of the joy that was waiting for Him." He was not ashamed of His criminal death on a tortuous wooden cross. Mocked and laughed at, taunted, "You saved others, but you cannot save yourself." (Mark 15:31 NIV)

He could have:

- Come down off that cross in a second.

- Ordered His mighty angel army to destroy the entire city of Jerusalem.

- Sent the Pharisees and the Sadducees to hell that very moment.

- Had the Roman soldiers crucified in the time it takes to say, "Do it".

But it didn't happen that way, because Jesus was obedient to His Father, submitting His own will to the will of His Father and surrendering Himself unto death, even the death on a cross.

He endured the suffering and the shame and believed in the *joy that was waiting for Him:*

- In the regal reunion of Father, Son, and Holy Spirit.

- In the triumphant homecoming in heaven.

- Where His Father had a throne in position and a crown in place.

- When the joy of the Father joined forces with the joy of His angels, and the entire heavenly host would sing,

   Worthy is the Lamb, who was slain, to receive power and wealth and wisdom and strength and honor and glory and praise! To Him who sits on the throne and to the Lamb, be praise and honor and glory and power. (Revelation 5:12–13 NIV)

I see Christian women, including myself, who cannot understand how to handle hurtful and even tragic circumstances in their lives or in the lives of their families, especially children and grandchildren.

Somehow, we feel betrayed by God. "I trusted God completely, I prayed diligently, I read His Word, I went to church, I served in the church, and now, because of my unmet expectations, I am deeply wounded. Where is the God I know in Scripture?"

Does this sound like you? It sounds like me. But God did not allow me to stay there. He taught me difficult truths in the grace of His love.

Here is God's mathematical equation when tragedy strikes.

> Total surrender of our circumstances, *plus* trust in the love and goodness of Jesus, *plus* hope in the heaven that awaits us, *equals* the pathway to complete joy.

And once we have the joy, His peace—the peace that surpasses all understanding—will keep our hearts and our minds in Christ Jesus. (Philippians 4:7 NIV)

Prayer

Jesus, Jesus, Jesus, what an example for us! What a love for us, that You endured the ravages of crucifixion, anticipating the joy that was waiting for You in heaven.

I humbly ask for strength in obedience, for an increase in faith and trust, and for a mind that puts my hope in heaven. Send a rich measure of Your Holy Spirit to let me rise above my circumstances, to have no expectations of my own, but simply rest in the sovereign choices that You make for my life.

Then I will rest in your joy and peace and presence. Thank you, Jesus, for Your great redemptive love, and thank You for staying on the cross to complete my salvation.

I love You, dearest Jesus, my Savior. Amen.

Keep Your Eyes on Jesus

Fix your eyes on Jesus—

Our Savior and our Lord.

When you think that you are failing,

Pray—your faith will be restored.

Fix your eyes on Jesus—

Example of faith and hope.

His life for us was perfect,

On the cross He gladly coped.

He surrendered all to Papa;

Gave up His throne in heaven, too.

And did it all for you, His child,

Died and paid the price for you.

He taught us to surrender all

Our worry, hurts, and pain.

Give it all to God's great plan,

True joy will be our gain.

—Elaine Kennelly

Dear _____, that is good advice—to fix your eyes on Me. Focus on being in My presence plus talking and listening to Me in prayer. I can bring order to your confusion and pain. I paid the price for your jail sentence in Hell. That is the truth, and with My truth, you will be set free!

Jesus

Day 14
Live One Day at a Time

*H*ere's a section of Scripture most of us already know. Matthew 6, starting at verse 9; it's the Lord's Prayer, and God taught me something I had never seen before in verse 11: "Give us this day our daily bread."

Here is the supernatural surprise of Scripture. We may have read a verse five hundred times through the years. We may have said it aloud hundreds of times and then, bingo, one day we actually learn something totally new from it.

That is how the Spirit of God works! He moves into our hearts through the power of Scripture working in our lives, showing us why we need to continue to read God's Word, especially as we get older.

God wants us to know, dear Something Sisters, that He is in charge of our lives, one day at a time, twenty-four hours per day. Only once did that change by a God-given miracle. Read Joshua 10: 12-14.

Speaking of creation, think about this. God gave us an example of living one day at a time.

Could he have created everything in one wave of His Hand? Yes, of course He could have, but He chose to work one day at a time.

Listen.

> Then God said, "Let there be light," and there was light ... then He separated the light from the darkness ... God called the light "Day" and the darkness "Night." And evening passed and morning came, making the first day. (Genesis 1:3–5 NLT)

Read the rest of the creation activities, and you will see that God created on each day for six days, and on the seventh day, He rested. That is how we are to live, and the very first book of the Bible shows us how.

Back to Matthew 6:11. "Give us this day our daily bread" is not just referring to food. What Jesus means here is "Give us *this* day what I need for *this* day."

Allow me, Jesus, to live within today with all of its

- Issues and schedules

- Troubles, fears, anxieties, pain, and unique circumstances

- Joys and blessings

So let's not get entangled in tomorrow's concerns, and let's not brood over yesterday's issues. Those words are easy to type onto the page, but they are difficult to live out.

Here is God's advice for living one day at a time:

- Trust Me for these twenty-four hours. Trust that I am walking next to you each step of each day. Look for Me. Listen to Me. Be expectant.

- Do not live in fear, since I am always with you. Fear drives you to excessive planning and impulsive actions. Give Me your daily fears and frustrations, and leave them with Me.

- I already know your needs for the day, and I can supply them, but I love to hear from you. Ask Me, talk to Me, pray to Me. I am the God of the universe. Do you really think I am unable or unwilling to supply the needs of My children? Hardly!

- When surprises come into your day, I already know about them, so please thank Me for each one. Thank Me even for the hurtful things that come in a day. It will change your perspective. I promise.

Here is a great way to pray. "God willing, I will see many tomorrows, but for today, Lord, please give me my daily day, with its problems and enjoyments and Your strength to cope with everything this day will bring."

For me, the results, after praying that way, have been less stress and a happier attitude, and an enjoyment for the work of today.

But here's the best result. Since type A personalities like me do not know when to quit, I now say, "I've done my day's daily work, and now I can do my day's daily enjoyment."

And there is still something new for me to do when I wake up tomorrow. God is good!

Prayer

My dearest friend, Jesus, thank You for giving each day just twenty-four hours, because You know that's all I can really handle. Thank You for planning the activities of each day and helping me realize I need not be in a frenzied state of activity every minute!

You are teaching me to rely on Your work schedule, Your energy, Your timing, and Your planning, and I am so grateful. I am a much happier person because I know You are in charge.

This may seem like such a small thing to learn, but for me, Lord, it has been huge. I know in my heart that I can relax in your schedule and still get a lot accomplished.

I offer my sincere appreciation for teaching an important life lesson. In Jesus' loving name I pray. Amen.

Today!

Lord, give me this day my daily bread.

But I do not mean for food to be fed.

No, I mean today, with its 24 hours,

Fill me especially with God's holy power.

Lord, walk beside me through every today,

So I may trust in Your presence and pray.

I do ask for all my needs to be met;

If I really trust You, there'll be no regret.

Today is the day that God's in control;

He is in charge of my heart and my soul.

He walks by my side; He's ever so near.

I give up my worries; I give up my fear.

Give me today what I should do for today,

And I will praise You every step of the way.

Help me to hold the hours—not by my plan,

But follow the guidance of Your loving hand.

—Elaine Kennelly

Dear _____, you get so entangled in the duties of the day you are worn to a frazzle by dinnertime. Come instead into My peace and My presence for relaxation and rest. My peace will melt away your worries and extreme planning. Stop fretting and start trusting. You will be a happier child of mine!

Jesus

Elaine and Christine, great friends and terrific business partners. (2012)

Day 15
How to Become a Conqueror

*a*s a child, I loved hearing about Jesus, and I loved to sing songs about Him. Oh, those wonderful hymns! At school, we even had to memorize some of them, which I didn't like at the time. But now I am very grateful for those stanzas that still pop out of my head when I sing in the shower.

In elementary school, one of my all-time favorites was "Stand Up, Stand Up for Jesus." Every time we sang it, we could stand up! And I was a "belter"—I would belt out those songs and didn't care what people thought of me.

Stand up, stand up for Jesus, Ye soldiers of the cross.

Lift high His royal banner; It must not suffer loss.

From victory unto victory, His army shall He lead,

'Til every foe is vanquished, And Christ is Lord indeed!

At eight years of age, I didn't really understand the battles we would have to fight every day of our lives. But I was ready to stand up for Jesus.

Ephesians 6:13–14 (NIV) talks a lot about standing.

> Therefore, put on the full armor of God, so that when the day of evil comes, you may be able to stand your ground, and after you have done everything, to stand. Stand firm then.

"Stand your ground" ... "to stand" ... "stand firm." Three times! God is calling us to action! My precious Something Sisters, you must get involved in your battle with Satan. Now is the time for action as we face a world of evil.

What exactly are we up against?

- Satan always lies to you. Every word he speaks is a lie.

- He and his demons daily accuse you, saying, "You are always wrong, stupid, fearful, worried, guilty." He accuses you with his lies!

- The world wants to choke out your faith with the importance of material things, possessions, and money.

- The world loves to beckon believers into evil strongholds of sin, such as pornography, lying, adultery, stealing, and addictions of all kinds.

- Our own flesh is all too eager to join into sin and evil practices.

That is what we are facing as individuals, couples, families, and even as a nation. We are in a battle with the powers of this dark world and spiritual forces of evil. And it is for real!

The Bible gives us a plan of action, and I can testify to its power, potency, and performance. It works, but you need to do it every day.

Put on the *full armor of God,* starting with your head.

Put on the *helmet of salvation.* I am ransomed, redeemed, and saved by the blood of Jesus Christ on the cross. It is finished, and Easter has confirmed it. The helmet covers your brain, the place where sinful thoughts keep swirling. Fill your mind with Scripture. How about Philippians 4:8–9?

Put on the *breastplate of righteousness*. Through Jesus Christ and His gift of salvation, I am in a right relationship with God.

When God sees me, He sees a perfect_____(put your name in the blank). The breastplate covers your heart, where all your motives are. Remember it is the wellspring of life. See Proverbs 4:23.

Put on the *belt of truth*. God's Word is absolute truth. It holds everything together, just like a belt or sash. Read John 14:6.

Your *feet should be ready.* I am sure-footed and firmly rooted in readiness to spread the Gospel message. Know the gospel, John 3:16.

Take up the *shield of faith*. My strong faith in Christ will extinguish *all* the flaming arrows of the evil one. "All"—I like that word. Every lie Satan tells me will be snuffed out by *my faith!* Read Romans 5:1.

Use the *sword of the Spirit*. Know, memorize, and use Scripture to refute Satan. If Jesus used Scripture against the Devil, so should we! Study Luke 4:1–12.

Pray in the Spirit, on all occasions, with all kinds of prayers and requests. Praying will keep you alert. And remember to pray for all believers.

Then, after the battle, you will be standing firm. Stand up, stand up for Jesus, ye Sisters of the cross!

Prayer

My dear heavenly Father, I am often lured into Satan's den of lies, hanging on pathetically to guilt, enjoying my prideful heart, and judging others unmercifully. Forgive my weaknesses. Keep me from temptation. Bind up Satan daily, and give me the power—Holy Spirit power—to resist him and all of his demons. Keep a hedge around my spouse, my children and grandchildren, and my friends, and protect them from evil.

I know without a doubt that I have victory in Jesus! His blood takes away all of my sins, guilt, pride, lust, greed, selfishness, and worldliness. I am redeemed.

Oh, dearest Savior, thankfulness flows from my heart to You. I am in a right relationship with You. Help me to lead a godly life, ready to battle Satan with Your help. I can do all things through Christ who strengthens me. (Philippians 4:13 NIV)

In His victorious name I pray. Amen.

You Have Power over Satan

In the book of James we are told we have power to resist.

I want you to know this, and I am going to insist!

Go ahead and read it now, it's James, chapter 4, verse 7.

Read aloud, and memorize it—use it as a lesson.

When Satan comes around and lies to you today,

You have a special tool to use; power comes your way.

The tool is very simple—resist the lies you think are cute.

Oppose him, assail him, every word by him dispute.

Refrain from even listening, counteract his evil lies,

By persisting, resisting, refuse to hear his evil cries.

Say, "Jesus, Jesus, Jesus," and order him to bow,

He will quickly flee from you, leave the room right now!

Oh, my friend, there is power in Jesus' name,

Just be prepared to use it.

On His name—just stake your claim!

Stand firm -- you'll never lose it.

—Elaine Kennelly

I have given you power to resist Satan, dear _____.
Just saying My name will show that you are resisting the
Devil, and he will flee from you. Please put My Word into
your memory so that you are prepared to fight the good
fight of faith. I will be with you every step of the way. Never
give up or give in!

Jesus

Day 16
Polar Events

*W*ell, this should grab your attention. Yes, I was born in Wisconsin, and I do often refer to it as the frozen tundra of the north. But today, we are not going to visit the North Pole or the South Pole.

Today we are going to visit opposites in character or action, and they are found in the Bible.

Kinda like oxymorons, those "figures of speech by which a locution produces an incongruous, seemingly self-contradictory effect." Did you get that? Wow, that's the fanciest definition I've seen in *www.dictionary.com*!

Here are a few that have caught my eye. I think all of us Something Sisters can relate to these found on *www.oxymoronlist.com*.

baggy tights

clean toilet

clearly confused

clogged drain

comfortable bra

considerate boss

diet ice cream

fresh frozen

minor disaster

objective parents

simple technology

sinfully good

There are also polar events in your life as a Christian woman. Did you ever try to worry and worship at the same time?

The Bible says a lot about worry, and all of it is convicting. It is a sin that has gotten a foothold in the way some Christian women think. I have found myself saying to our son, Nathan, "It's a mother's job to worry." Ouch!

No, it is not a mother's job to worry, nor anyone else's job who professes to be a Christian. Worry is a sin! But somehow, Satan, the world, and my own mind have infiltrated my thinking to believe it is a positive thing to worry about loved ones, especially children, grandchildren, or elderly parents.

Psalm 37 (NIV) is a wonderful piece of advice from God! "Do not fret ... Do not fret ... Trust in the Lord and do good ... do not fret ... enjoy great peace."

Matthew 6:34 (NIV) reads, "Therefore, do not worry about tomorrow, for tomorrow will worry about itself. Each day has enough trouble of its own." In other words, today's trouble is enough for today.

Oh, Something Sisters, it is not a badge of honor to worry. We have been lied to, and we have bought into it. It's time to stop anguish, apprehension, doubt, despair, and distress and trust in the Lord with all our hearts (Proverbs 3:5).

When anxiety does get a hold on you, the best antidote is worshipping God, adoring Jesus, thanking Him for salvation, bowing down in reverence and awe to our generous Father, exalting the name of the Lord, and loving and lauding the Holy Spirit and His power.

Just raise your hands to heaven, and give gratitude to God! Pray to Him, thanking Him for everything, even the problems and troubles we may have. Esteem His holiness. Sing to the God of the universe. Confess your worry to Him, and ask Him for His peace. Venerate the Trinity—Father, Son, and Holy Spirit.

Real worship will give us power to overcome perceived problems. You know what, dear Something Sisters? God gave us a brain. Let's use it.

Your worshipful thoughts will free you from the bondage of bad news and biting nails.

Prayer

Thank You, Holy Spirit, for convicting me of worry. You have always proven Yourself to be generous, worthy of my trust, providing all that I need, and yet I succumb to anxiety, worrying, and fretting. Worrying causes my mind to be swirling, and I find that to be counterproductive.

Help me to trust You one day at a time!

Holy Spirit, please keep me from thinking that my worrying will help in any way. I have bought into the lie that I am showing my love for someone if I worry over them.

How misguided I have been. Thank You for Your Word and for the Holy Spirit living in me. Without the Spirit's guidance, I would be left to my own pitiful self. How beautiful it is to be loved by You, my gracious God, Father, Son, Holy Spirit.

Release women everywhere from the bondage of worry, and rid their minds of useless anxiety and excessive fear. Instead, encourage us all to worship You, trust You, and give praise and thanksgiving to Your Holy name!

In the powerful name of Jesus and His Spirit. Amen.

In Praise of the Trinity

I love you Lord,

I love you with all my heart.

I love you from the depths of my soul.

I could not love you more.

I could not love you more.

Father, I adore you,

I profess my adoration.

I profess my worship.

You are worthy of my praise.

You are worthy of so much more.

Jesus, you are everything.

You are everything to me.

You are Salvation!

You are Redemption!

You are more than everything I need.

Spirit of God, You are Holy.

Oh, so Holy is everything You are.

Surround me. Live in me.

You are my Source of faith and life.

I could not need you more.

The Trinity is Three-in-One,

And One-in-Three is He.

They are in Relationship,

Relationship with me.

I could not ask for more.

—Elaine Kennelly

My precious _____, worry is useless, and it will only take you into darkness. Instead, come to Me, and come into the light. Bring me your problems and all your life circumstances, so I can take them off your mind and heart. I can refresh your spirit and give you rest. Come to Me today!

Love, Jesus

Day 17
Suffering

*J*esus could not have said it any clearer: "In this world you will have trouble" (John 16:33 NIV). Seven words that really do affect every person on earth.

Years ago I quoted Max Lucado in my journal: "Trying to avoid suffering in this life is like trying to avoid breathing. It can't be done. As a matter of fact, the Bible says that those who desire to live a godly lifestyle will suffer."

Suffering is being in some kind of pain, distress, agony, or torment.

"Pain is whatever the experiencing person says it is, existing when ever and where ever the person says it does. No one can tell another person that they are not in pain," says Margo McCaffery, whose job is pain research.

http://en.wikipedia.org/w/index.php?title=Margo_ McCaffery&oldid+491309804

What kinds of pain are there?

- Relational pain—divorce, parent abandonment, prodigal children, unreturned love

- Physical pain—diseases such as arthritis, cancer, Parkinson's, migraine headaches

- Emotional pain—where loss is involved,
  such as a death, loss of job, loss of home,
  disappointment

- Spiritual pain—great fear, unusual doubt, heavy
  guilt, feeling separated from God or ignored by
  Him, not understanding God's love for you

The life of Joseph in the book of Genesis is one of the most encouraging messages from God. If you look at the kinds of pain listed above, Joseph had them all. God allows Joseph's story to teach us how to endure.

Joseph lived in a dysfunctional family before that term was ever created. Of course, a family composed of one husband, two wives—Leah and Rachel—two concubines—Bilhah and Zilpah—twelve sons, and I don't know how many daughters … how could it not be dysfunctional?

The biblical account of Joseph starts when he is seventeen years old. Remember that. Out of the twelve boys, Joseph is second-youngest, and he tattles on his ten older brothers, "bringing Jacob a bad report about them" (Genesis 37:2 NIV).

It also states that his father, Jacob, gave Joseph a beautiful coat of many colors, while all the other brothers got … nothing.

Of course, the brothers "hated [Joseph] and would not speak kindly about him" (Genesis 37:4).

To make matters worse, Joseph had dreams indicating the brothers, and even dear ol' Dad would bow down and pay homage to none other than Joseph himself! Not bad to have the dreams, but Joseph eagerly told the entire family about them—not exactly a way to win friends and influence people. "His brothers are jealous" (verse 11) and plot to kill him. Here's the rest of the story in condensed form.

- They plot to kill him out in the fields while
  tending the family flocks. Jacob had sent Joseph

out there to check on things. Obviously, Jacob was clueless.

- Reuben (the oldest) gets them to agree to just throw Joseph into a cistern, minus the ornamental robe, of course.

- A caravan headed for Egypt comes by, and the brothers sell Joseph into slavery, while Reuben is not present.

- The ten evil brothers take the coat, dip it into goat's blood, and give it to their elderly father, saying, "Poor Joseph is dead, evidently killed by a wild animal."

- Joseph lands a slave position in the house of Potiphar.

- But he is seduced by Potiphar's conniving wife, and when Joseph spurns her, he gets thrown into prison, even though he is totally innocent.

- He remains in prison for over two years.

- And he doesn't land a new job until he is thirty years old.

Joseph suffered all kinds of pain for thirteen years: attempted murder; being hated and sold into slavery by his own family; moved hundreds of miles away; and enduring slavery, seduction, lies, false imprisonment. Even his own father did not know the real truth about Joseph for over twenty years! It had to affect Joseph's thoughts and actions.

Read the remainder of Genesis, and stop at chapter 50:20. Joseph is speaking. "You intended to harm me, but God intended it for good to accomplish what is now being done, the saving of many lives."

Read it twice, three times. I had to ... I was stunned by how Joseph trusted God, waited for God to act, and never talked about how he was victimized!

Where are you on the path of "suffering"? You are on one, you know. We all have just gotten on, are walking through, or just gotten off the path of pain.

How are you processing your suffering? That is where we need to do better, my Something Sisters. The world is watching how we Christians react to pain, sorrow, loss, lies, unfair treatment, and ridicule. What does your track record look like? Does your life scream, "I'm a victim," or are you strong enough in your faith to say, "I trust you, dear Jesus"?

Yes, it can be instant or take many years, but God uses our suffering and pain to accomplish His desires and His purposes.

Sounds like Romans 8:28 (NLT): "We know that God causes everything to work together for the good of those who love God and are called according to His purpose for them."

As Christian women, all of us are just ordinary people who have been made extraordinary by God's purpose for them.

Be a Josephina!

Prayer

Almighty Father, thirteen years is a long time to suffer, but You did not call it suffering, did You? It was Joseph's training ground to become second-in-charge in the entire country of Egypt. To become; we are always becoming, aren't we, Father?

Sometimes I resist Your training tactics. I don't want to suffer, to heal, to work feelings through, to process my pain. I just want You to "fix it." I think most of us just want You to fix it and make it go away.

Help us to be like Joseph, who trusted. I'm sure he was hurting, but the Bible does not say he complained about his circumstances or grumbled about how unfair life was or what a rotten deal he had been dealt. Poor Joseph, poor me.

Father, I want a heart like Joseph's, a faith like Joseph's, a positive attitude like Joseph's! Help us all, dear Jesus, to learn from our suffering and become the women of faith *You* desire us to be!

With Your power, we can heal and become Your delight! Amen and Amen!

Processing the Path of Pain

Living on this earth holds a promise, that's for sure.

Jesus plainly told us we'd have troubles to endure.

So when your life is shattered by tragedy and pain,

Remember, it's a process for peace to be regained.

It's not easy, but you need to acknowledge pain exists.

Since pride does not admit that anguish still persists.

We stuff those painful feelings into our heart with ease,

And put on our "Happy Face," so others we can please.

Now listen very carefully—do not be led astray—

Those feelings "stuffed" inside just do not go away.

They slowly penetrate your mind, your very soul.

They eat at you, eventually they take their cruel toll.

You end up in a place called Bitterness and Shame.

Satan tells you constantly, "You're the one to blame."

Your life is wrapped in fear, dismay, and worry,

As you begin to doubt; "Does God really love me?"

I've gone this way, down this self-defeating path,

Thinking I was to blame and deserving of God's wrath.

Then said a voice inside of me, _____, these words are true:

"Know without a doubt,

your heavenly Father still loves you."

It took me years of prayer and reading of God's Word

To understand that God loves me. My salvation is secured.

Slowly I was able to deal with my feelings and my pain,

Delighting in God's Love for me, my Peace came back again.

—Elaine Kennelly

My purpose for you, dear child, _____, is not to avoid trouble and pain but to produce a faith strong enough to endure and overcome your suffering. I have never said that life would be easy. What I did say is that I come easily into your life to give faith, strength, power, and resistance to temptation. Just ask Me to come in!

All my love, Jesus

Day 18
Followship

*N*ope, it is not a typo. I mean followship. The opposite of leadership.

I scanned Amazon and found hundreds of books on leadership, but only one on followship, and the word used was *followership*.

What is followship? It is the art of following. I think it is the lost art of following. It is following someone, something, or some belief.

Something Sisters, let's see what the Bible has to say about following. Using my NIV Concordance, I found 388 entries under "follow," "followers," "following," "followed."

In the Old Testament, God uses "follow" or some form of follow many times, because He is directing the Israelites to follow Him and the many commands and statutes He gives. Over and over He says, "Do not follow other gods. Do follow My commands."

In the New Testament, Jesus also uses the word "follow" or "followers."

- "Follow Me," He said to his disciples.

- Jesus said, "Take up your cross and follow Me."

- Jesus said, "Whoever serves me must follow me."

- Revelation 17:14 (NIV) says, "They will wage war against the Lamb, but the Lamb will triumph over them because He is Lord of Lords and King of Kings—and with Him will be His called, chosen and faithful followers."

Why do I even bring this up? Why did God put it on my heart to write about following?

Because over and over again in Scripture, it says we are to follow Jesus. We are to follow the commands of God. We are to follow as the Spirit leads us. As Christians, we are followers of the Lord Jesus Christ!

First of all, it is a *privilege* to follow Jesus. We are His chosen children! Doesn't that make you feel special?

Today on a bumper sticker I saw, "I was born right the first time. OK?" obviously taking offense to the phrase "born again." I felt so sorry for the driver. He sees no need for the love of God, for a Savior, for redemption, and ultimately the best gift of all—eternity with the King of Kings.

In my heart, I know that when I stand before God at the judgment seat of Christ, I will have to account for my life with all its sin and flaws. But then the precious arms of Jesus will enfold me, and He will dress me in the white robe of righteousness created for each of His redeemed children.

God will look at me and see … perfection. I call that a privilege. Enjoy!

Second, by following Jesus, I receive the *power* of the Holy Spirit. Doesn't that make you feel strong?

The psalmist says, "When I called, you answered me. You made me bold and stout-hearted." (Psalm 138:3 NIV).

Paul writes in Romans 8:26 (NIV), "In the same way, the Spirit helps us in our weakness. We do not know what we ought to pray, but the Spirit himself intercedes for us … in accordance with God's will."

God's Spirit makes me powerful.

If you know the story of the apostle Paul, God changed him from the inside out in one laser beam. Zap! Off that horse and on to the journey of a lifetime. He is often called the greatest missionary to have ever lived.

Let's go to 2 Corinthians 12:7 (NLT). Paul is telling us about a problem he has, a, "thorn in his flesh, a messenger from Satan to torment me and keep me from being proud." Paul also tells us he prayed about it and *begged God* to "take it away."

Listen to God's word-by-word answer. "_____, My grace is all you need. My power works best in weakness" (2 Corinthians 12:9 NLT). Be sure to put your name in the blank.

All of us are weak. There is not one woman in all the world who is strong outside of being in Christ Jesus. But if the power of Christ is working in you, my precious Something Sister, you are strong, and God will accomplish much through your life, one day at a time.

We follow Jesus because He has a *purpose* for our lives.

Here is another area where God shows me my thinking has been faulty. For years, I thought God's purpose for my life was a project or a dream, like becoming a teacher or mother, owning a business, or writing a book.

No, these are *my* projects, not that God doesn't take delight in these outcomes or activities. Yet, God's purpose for our lives is the process of life itself.

His purpose for me is to depend on Him, one day at a time, trusting in His power now. The process is where God accomplishes His purpose for my life.

After the suicide of our eighteen-year-old son, Matthew, my life became void of God. I am not proud of the choices I made at the time, dear Something Sisters, because I shut God out of my life. Oh, I still went to church, but I refused to listen, counting the ceiling tiles instead.

For nine years, I tried to isolate myself from God, building high and thick walls around myself, and God did not interrupt the process. Remember, God is a gentleman and does not force Himself on us. We do have free-will.

I put on my happy face and stuffed all my hurts inside.

However, through those nine to ten years, I came to the point—in church, of all places—where I heard the pastor talk about the solace of God. I actually opened my ears and my heart to one word: "solace." Such an odd word. Who uses "solace" in conversation these days? But I *heard* it.

Guess what? I missed the solace of Jesus in my life. My thick walls of isolation made my heart like a stone. And I didn't want to be a stone! I was tired of being bitter and empty and hard.

The process of healing was God's purpose for my life for all those years. Today is still God's purpose for my life. Now is the training ground. Today is how I show God I am accomplishing His purposes for my life.

I want you, dear Something Sisters, to really think about that.

Prayer

Dear Jesus, You are my leader, and I am thrilled to be following You. You have the answers for eternal life, and I give thanks to You and praise Your Holy name.

I am privileged to be Your child, protected and blessed each day of my life. I know that I receive power following You. Send Your Holy Spirit each day to make me bold, to give me comfort, to teach me to pray, to be strengthened in my faith, and to inspire me to be a blessing to others.

I love You, Jesus, and I love living in the Light of Your presence. You are the Light of the world, and when You shine on me, You fill me with love that I can pass on to others. I am so happy when I allow Your presence to take charge of my life. I give my life to You completely. I work in You, and I rest in You. You are my all in all! There is nothing that I need when I live in Your presence.

All praise and thanks go to You. I will follow You every day of my life and then You will lovingly take me home into Your glorious presence in heaven. In Jesus' name. Amen.

My Presence Awaits You

Bring your problems into My Presence.

I'm here, loving you, for sure.

Bring your sins, and lay them at the cross;

My Forgiveness makes you pure.

Bring your questions into My Presence.

I will answer what you ask.

Bring your prayers to my altar;

Giving of Myself is a lovely task.

Bring your weariness into My Presence.

I provide Solace—needed Rest.

Bring your tired mind and spirit;

Healing souls is what I do best.

Bring yourself into My Presence.

You need quiet time, a quiet place.

Above all, bring your listening heart

To receive my Glorious Grace!

Come into the Light of My Presence.

With My Peace, I set you free

To receive all I would love to give

As you put your trust in Me.

—Elaine Kennelly

Dear _____, My heart's desire is for you to follow Me all the days of your life. I know everything there is to know about you, and I love you anyway. I will send My Holy Spirit to strengthen you, and if you believe in Me, you shall live in the Light of My Presence, where there is peace and rest.

Follow Me, Jesus

Day 19
God's Fashion Show

*W*e have had our beauty treatment, so now it's on to a fashion show. Who says that God's Word is no longer relevant? Those who feel that way are just not reading with open hearts!

In my *Life Application Study Bible,* page 2153, there is a great opening paragraph on the book of Colossians:

> Remove the head coach, and the team flounders;
>
> Break the fuel line, and the car won't run;
>
> Unplugged, the electrical appliance has no power;
>
> Without the head, the body dies.
>
> Whether for leadership, power, or life, connections are vital.

Colossians is a book of connections.

Paul, the author of this letter, writes about being connected with Christ through faith, and how important it is for believers to stay connected with each other, as in the body of Christ.

I think you will enjoy this and learn much about how to put your faith into action. After all, faith must be lived where we work, in our neighborhood, with our families, with our friends, and in the marketplace.

> Don't lie to one another. You're done with that old life. It's like a filthy set of ill-fitting clothes you've stripped off and put in the fire. (Colossians 3:9 The Message)

Paul had just written about what it is like to live now as a Christian, telling the new believers that their old, immoral life is dead. Their new life in Christ is alive, and that means killing off all their old, sinful habits.

Listen to how Paul describes those sinful habits.

> Sexual promiscuity, impurity, lust, doing whatever you feel like, whenever you feel like it, and grabbing whatever attracts your fancy. That's a life shaped by things and feelings instead of by God. (Colossians 3:5 The Message)

Wow! Sounds like America, right now: Internet pornography, sexually explicit movies, friends with "benefits," and filthy language used everywhere. (I went online for texting abbreviations and was stunned by the filth!)

Jump ahead to verses 12–14.

> So, chosen by God for this new life of love, dress in the wardrobe God picked out for you:
>
> > Compassion, kindness, humility, quiet strength, discipline. Be even-tempered, content with second place, quick to forgive an offense. Forgive as quickly and completely as the Master forgave you. And regardless of what else you put on, wear love. It's your basic, all-purpose garment. Never be without it.

God "picked out" the garments, but *you* must "put them on."

When our children and grandchildren were very young, we had to put their clothes on for them. But as they matured, they put on what they chose. (Had a few arguments, did you?)

Well, God is our Father, and as baby believers, He sent His Spirit to encourage and assist. Now we are adult believers, and God still empowers us with the Holy Spirit, and He will help. God tells us point blank, "you must clothe yourselves" (NIV), "put on" (HCSB), "you must clothe yourselves" (NLT), "put on" (NKJV), "clothe yourselves" (AMP). We cannot escape this direct command by God.

If we deliberately choose to ignore God, we are back in the garden of Eden and our names are Eve. Satan is telling us lies that sound like this: "Forgive her? Never, she hurt my feelings, and I will never speak to her again."

Or maybe something like this: "I am just too busy to call today. I'll wait until the funeral is over and everything quiets down. I'll call then."

Or maybe, " I hate him! I was overlooked, and that promotion belongs to me. I deserve it! I'll do everything in my power to make him look bad."

When Satan whispers those lies, have some ammunition ready:

- As I stand outside or inside my closet, choosing an outfit, I will say out loud, "Today I am going to clothe myself with *compassion.*"

- As I step into my jeans, I will say out loud, "Today I am going to put on *kindness.*"

- As I slide a top over my head, I will say out loud, "Today I am going to *be humble.*"

- As the belt goes through the loops, I will say out loud, "Today I am going to have *strength through Christ Jesus.*"

- As I look at my shoe rack, I will say, "Today I will choose *discipline.*"

- Right shoe, "Today I will be *even-tempered,* no angry flare-ups."

- Left shoe, "I will be *content with second place* all day."

- My watch goes on the wrist, and I say, "I will be *quick to forgive* others, just as Jesus has forgiven me. Every time I glance at my watch throughout the day, I will say, 'Help me, sweet Jesus, to forgive others as you have forgiven me.'"

- I grab my purse, which completes the outfit. It's something I always take with me, and I say out loud, "*I intend to love everyone who comes into my path today!*"

What did we tell our children? "The more you do it, the easier it gets!" Plus we have the power of God to help us. Call on Him. Ask Him for help. Do you know who lives inside of you? The powerful Holy Spirit of God.

God changes us from the inside out. It starts in our mind, goes to our heart, and ends up in action. Pray and ask God to help you. He will.

It is one of God's great guarantees.

Prayer

Heavenly Father, Help me! Pour out Your Holy Spirit power on me right now. I sin with my brain and my heart, so nobody sees it. I come across as a pretty good Christian, but inside, I am not. Please forgive me.

I need to be changed from the inside out, Father. I want to be compassionate and kind. I want to be self-disciplined. I want to forgive and forget. I want to be more loving to the people around me ... starting with my husband and family.

As I get dressed each day, remind me of Your words. As I go to work, bring these words to mind. Help me to memorize Your clothing for me. Then help me choose to wear them boldly, consistently, and lovingly.

I know with Your help all things are possible! I love you. Amen.

God's Wardrobe for Us

In Colossians 3, verse 12,

God talks to all of us today.

He gives us current fashion tips:

What to wear for work and play.

He says that we are chosen

For this brand-new life of love.

He does not say we need to wear

Costly clothes and fancy gloves.

No, we need to wear the wardrobe

Picked by God for us to wear.

He's chosen very carefully.

Put on each piece with prayer.

First—put on sweet compassion,

Then kindness from your heart.

Add humility—no pride for us at all.

Pride keeps friendships far apart.

We now can add strong discipline,

Then on God's path we will stay.

Be even-tempered, don't explode.

Have much patience on display.

Please be content with second place;

Forgive an offense then forget.

Just as the Master has forgiven us,

Reach out and cancel all those debts.

Regardless of what else we wear

Let's put on the dress of love.

It's our all-purpose garment

Given by God above!

Love—never be without it.

Let's wear it every day.

It will bring us Blessedness

And Joy along our way.

—Elaine Kennelly

My dear,_____, I am pleased when your faith is evident by your actions. I do expect you, as My believing and saved child, to live with the garments I have chosen for you to wear. These pieces of clothing are not optional. A child of Mine lives wearing all of them!

Jesus

Day 20
The 4G Network

his topic would not even have been possible just a few years ago. Who knows? This may be the first devotional to discuss the 4G network.

We've all heard the hype, but what actually is it? Here is what I found by going to *www.cellphones.about.com.*

> 4G wireless is the term used to describe the fourth-generation of wireless service.
>
> No matter what technology is behind it, 4G wireless is designed to deliver speed. On average, 4G wireless is supposed to be anywhere from four to ten times faster than today's 3G networks. Sprint says its 4G WiMax network can offer download speeds that are ten times faster than a 3G connection, with speeds that top out at 10 megabits per second. Verizon's LTE network, meanwhile, can deliver speeds between 5 mbps and 12 mbps.
>
> 4G is only available in limited areas.

Ahhh, the power of wireless services. I'm sure you all understood every word you read.

Here is the truth about cell phones from one Something Sister to another: we do not understand the technology behind it, but we sure do depend on it, don't we?

The other day, my husband handed me a slip of paper. Written on it was, "The 4G Network—God-Given Grace

Guaranteed." He said, "I think you should write a poem about that!" And since I obey my husband all the time (cough, cough), we owe today's devotion to Tom for his great idea.

God-given grace guaranteed. From one Something Sister to another, we do not understand the theology behind it, but we sure do depend on it, don't we?

We could add another G and have the 5G Network—gift! God is always ahead of the curve, isn't He?

> But God is so rich in mercy, and He loved us so much that even though we were dead because of our sins, He gave us life when He raised Christ from the dead, and God saved you by His grace when you believed. And you can't take credit for this; it is a gift from God. Salvation is not a reward for the good things we have done, so none of us can boast about it. (Ephesians 2:4–5, 8–9 NLT)

To my best friends, if there is one message that this book engraves into your mind and into your heart, I hope it is this: God loves you very much, and He has a gift for you, and it's called grace—God's redemption at Christ's expense.

Jesus died on the cross for you and me. All of our sins are forgiven when we believe in the Lord Jesus Christ. It is a gift that lasts forever, because when you die as a believer, God takes you home to be with Him for all eternity.

If you go back to the definition of the wireless 4G network, it states in the last paragraph, "4G is only available in limited areas." Do I have good news for you! God's 5G network is available *everywhere* and to *everyone*. No one is too old or too young. No one is too smart or too dull. No one has sinned so much that they cannot be forgiven, and no one is too perfect that they do not need God's grace.

Jesus is waiting for you right now to give you His gift. Just cup your hands together, reach them out to God, and say, "Yes, Jesus, I need your gift today. Sign me up for your 5G network. I accept the terms of Your service—it's free, it's forever, and it's final. I am Your redeemed child. I believe."

Then click on submit.

Prayer

Dear Jesus, I am not always sure how to pray. I'm not sure if I am doing this correctly, but I do know that tears are streaming down my face. I know without a doubt that I need a Savior. I need forgiveness. I need Your gift of grace.

It's like opening a present, and inside is a miracle. I don't understand it, but I sure do need it, and I promise to depend on You for the rest of my life. I feel as though a burden has been lifted from me, and I can take a really deep breath for the first time in my life.

Thank you for this relief and for Your promise of heaven. And while I'm still here on earth, help me to grow in my trust of You and my faith in You.

I know You will. Thank you for loving me so much. Amen.

God's 5G Network

God is the subject

Of this little heartfelt poem.

He gives me life and after death,

He will take me Home.

Something Sisters

Given is the verb,

The lovely action that God does.

He gives me all I need to live,

He blesses as He loves.

Grace is God's gift to me

Through Christ upon the cross.

Grace frees me from the wrath of sin.

I will not suffer loss.

Guaranteed means God has

promised. It will happen as He said.

All I must do is trust Him;

On His Word I'm daily fed.

The fifth G stands for *Gift*,

On God's Network you'll find Grace;

This gift is yours, you have been saved,

The cross—Christ took your place.

That means you are God's precious child

If only you believe.

Open up your heart to Jesus,

And this great blessing you'll receive.

God's Network is the worldwide church,

Made up of sinners, just like me.

But sinners who now trust in Christ,

And receive His Grace for free.

—Elaine Kennelly

Grace is the best gift you can receive from Me, _____. I have paid your debt to God in full. It is finished. There is nothing you can do to earn your forgiveness, and you certainly are not good enough just by going to church to pave your pathway to heaven. I am the Way, the Truth, and the Life.

Jesus

Beth and Elaine; a former client turns into a very best friend, who shares her art talents with Elaine. They also go to the same church. (2012)

Day 21
A + N + B = God's Will

I counted fifteen meanings and connotations for the word *will*. Why the big fuss? Because it is not a "wheel."

During my first church service in the South, I heard all about God's wheel. I did, yes, ma'am! It actually took me a couple of minutes to figure it all out. I'm from Wisconsin, remember?

So God's will is used here as a noun. It is His declaration, His direction, His decree, and His demand. Guess what? It's not optional.

God's words are always definitive—it's all or none, or always or never. God does not make things complicated. We do that quite well on our own, thank you.

Let's go to the New Testament letter of 1 Thessalonians.

It was written by the apostle Paul to the church at Thessalonica. The church was maybe two or three years old, so Paul wrote a letter of encouragement, inspired by the Holy Spirit.

God sends us this same letter of encouragement. Read chapter 5, verses 16–18. I'm using the New Living Translation, because it is easy to memorize.

Always be joyful.

Never stop praying.

> Be thankful in all circumstances, for this is God's will for you who belong to Christ Jesus.

Volumes have been written, sermons preached, and debates conducted through the centuries over what really is the will of God.

And here is the very simple, truthful declaration from God.

Always + Never + Be = God's Will for Us

Always Be Joyful + Never Stop Praying + Be Thankful

in All Circumstances

That is God's will for you who belong to Christ Jesus.

I am going to confess something about myself, my Something Sisters: I have agonized over what God's will is for my life. I had it blown so out of proportion. I made it such a big deal, and God makes it very simple to understand.

Oh, did I say, "Easy to do"? No, I said, "Very simple to understand."

First, God says, "Always be joyful," and that means in good times and in not-so-good times. Joy comes from your head, your thoughts. You think joy. You pray joy (Philippians 1:3 NIV).

The truth of God's Word ministers to our minds in these moments. If you are depending on feelings, dear friends, joy will be "iffy," because feelings are "iffy."

Something Sisters, your joy will only come naturally if you know God's Word, that is why memorizing is so crucial to your everyday walk with God.

C. S. Lewis said, "Joy is the serious business of heaven." Ask God for His thoughts on joy. Ask Him to help you to discover joy. That is a godly request, and He will do it.

Our attitude should be one of joy. Christian women need to smile more and laugh louder! Remember, "A smile is a curve that sets things straight" (Author unknown).

Second, God says, "Never stop praying." Now that is interesting. How do we do that? We are still out in public. We still go to jobs. We still have phone calls and TV. (Well, we could skip the TV.)

When we have Jesus in our minds and our hearts, our thoughts are prayers. Our attitudes are prayers. Our love to others are prayers.

I heard Founder of Insight for Living Ministry, Chuck Swindoll, say once that we pray like a "hacking cough." It's just there. It's spontaneous! Prayer is just talking to God.

I think prayer is equivalent to our thought patterns. Our thoughts, singing, laughter, and smiling are all prayers that continually go before the Lord. Remember that, and you will be praying all the time.

Third, be thankful not *for* every circumstance but *in* every circumstance. There is a big difference. Remember the back of the tapestry. Threads are going every which way, and they make no sense. But the front of the tapestry is beautiful and makes total sense. Give God thanks in all circumstances, because He sees, knows, and understands the back of the tapestry as well as the front.

Jesus is deserving of our joy, our prayers, and our thanks. We have a good God!

Prayer

Dear Jesus, my friend, I'm so glad that I can call You my friend. Friends talk together a lot. Friends share ideas, thoughts, concerns, and troubles. Thank You for explaining

Your will for my life. I do understand it better, and I am going to memorize that equation.

Help me through the power of the Holy Spirit to think joy in my everyday life. Help me to pray more often—not necessarily long, fancy prayers like this but short thoughts I share with you. Let me see joy in the circumstances of my life. I do need to smile and laugh much more!

Precious Jesus, thank You for loving me so much. Even in my moments of hurt and sadness, I can see Your loving arm holding me up. You will never let the righteous fall, and I can sing in the shadow of Your wings. Your right hand will guide me and hold me fast. Thank You, loving Father. In Jesus' name. Amen.

Always + Never + Be

God's Word is very simple;

God makes it very clear.

It's me who makes it difficult.

It's me who looks in fear.

Am I listening to God?

Do I know His will for sure?

Am I spending time with Him?

Do I have a heart that's pure?

"Silly Child," God just smiles.

"My love is not based on skills.

I never look at you and scoff.

And say, 'She knows not My will.'

Here's my message sent to you.

It's plain, as you can see.

You will know My will for you,

Just remember A + N + B."

—Elaine Kennelly

My will for you, _____, is that your life would be full of joy, that you would talk to Me every day, many times, and that you would thank Me in whatever circumstances make up your day. Remember, live one day at a time. I will never leave you or forsake you. Why, I live inside of you! That itself should bring you joy.

Love, Jesus

Day 22
The Little Gray Cells

a gatha Christie was a prolific British author, and I loved reading her mystery novels. I still enjoy reading them for the second or third time. That's one of the benefits of being "mature" and blond.

One of her most popular characters is the Belgian detective Hercule Poirot. He always attributed his marvelous success at solving crimes to the use of his "little gray cells." He often remarked to his partner, Captain Hastings, "It is the brain, the little gray cells on which one must rely. One must seek the truth within—not without." Little did Agatha Christie realize what a biblical truth that statement was.

The brain, the "little gray cells," holds the power for Christians. I think Satan has led us astray from "thoughts of our brain" to "feelings of the heart"—to emotions rather than clear thinking.

First Corinthians 2:11 (NLT) holds many teachings on thoughts, especially the thoughts of God.

> No one can know a person's thoughts except that person's own spirit, and no one can know God's thoughts except God's own Spirit. And we have received God's Spirit (not the world's spirit), so we can know the wonderful things God has freely given us.

> When we tell you these things, we do not use words that come from human wisdom. Instead, we speak words given to us by the Spirit, using the Spirit's words to explain spiritual truths. (1 Corinthians 2:10b–13)

The Holy Spirit knows the mind of God because He is God, and it is through the Holy Spirit that we learn the truths from God. The Holy Spirit tells us what's on God's mind, what God is thinking. God's thoughts can become our thoughts!

You want to really know God? Then know His words, because they contain His thoughts.

Consider this:

> Because of [God's] glory and excellence, He has given us great and precious promises. These are the promises that enable you to share His divine nature. (2 Peter 1:4 NLT)

We can absolutely and genuinely share God's divine nature through His promises to us. That sentence contains fabulous truths for us, and where are those promises?

They are in the Bible!

Here is an "Ouch!" statement, because it hurts me to have to put this into words. Dearest Something Sisters, we are weak Christians, because we do not have God's words etched into our minds.

When our emotions are in a feel-good state, our brain thinks pleasant thoughts. But when our emotions are in a state of fear, anger, anxiety, sorrow, pride, or depression, then what?

In order for our faith and trust to grow, we must think the thoughts of God, through the power of the Holy Spirit.

It's called head knowledge. When we have a sore on our arm, we put a bandage on it. But when we have a sore in our soul, we need the knowledge of God in our mind to protect us, just like a bandage.

Remember, Satan lies to us. We must combat that by telling Satan the truth. Where is the truth? In God's Word. But do we always have a copy of the Bible with us? Oh, it could be in our cell phone, which is handy.

But God's Word is closest when it is already in our brain. We have it there through the process of memory.

Look at Jesus. When Satan came to Him in the wilderness in Luke 4:1–12, what did Jesus do? He quoted Scripture every time Satan spoke to Him. Look at verse 13: "When the devil had finished all this tempting, he left Him until an opportune time."

An opportune time? If Satan went back again and again to Jesus, what do you think Satan does with us?

I am begging you to take this seriously. We, as Something Sisters over fifty years of age, need to learn what is in the Bible.

Our pastor, Dr. Jimmy Jackson, often says, "We are just one generation away from losing Jesus in our country." My desire for you is sincere, and it is serious. I want women all over the world to know God's Word and, "to be saved and to come to a knowledge of the truth" (1 Timothy 2:4 NIV).

And God's truth needs to be in our minds. Always! Forever! Yes, I believe many mature women are children of God, and now they need to grow up to be *mature in their faith*.

Why do we not memorize Scripture? I think we are too busy. I think we do not take God seriously in our lives. I think we don't find God and His Word to be of value. I think an intimate relationship with Jesus Christ is not a priority for many of us.

We have all these excuses, "Oh, I'll do that tomorrow." "Too busy today." "Oh, I just can't memorize anything anymore." "Must be getting too old."

But we can do it! We *can* grow in our faith. Please, don't be lazy when it comes to your relationship with God.

Today—read God's Word and memorize just one verse. I challenge you.

Prayer

Forgive me for my apathy, Father. Help me to want to read Your words. I know that many days, I do not put You first in my life. I let so many other things crowd You out of my thinking. I am so sorry, and I do repent of my laziness.

Energize me through Your Word. Speak the Holy Spirit to me, giving me power to take action—reading my Bible and memorizing passages. I want to grow stronger in my faith and discipline.

In fact, dear Jesus, I want to make a decision right now. This Sunday I will go to church. Today I will read my Bible. Today I will pray. It's really kind of funny. How do I expect to grow in my faith if I do not read Your Word or go to church?

Change my way of thinking. Please! I want to make my relationship with You top priority. I do love You, Lord, and thank You for reminders, just like this devotional.

In Jesus' name I pray. Amen.

God Is My Priority

God gave me His precious Bible.

It is beautiful in my sight.

How wonderful are His words to me.

They are my pure delight.

But if I do not read His Word,

And I never open up the Book,

Will it still be wonderful for me,

If I never open it and look?

If I choose to leave it on the shelf

And never go to church,

How will I ever grow my faith?

How will His truth reveal my search?

I must make God a priority and

Read His Word every day.

I must tuck the truth into my mind,

Do it NOW—and don't delay.

If I keep my word and read His Word,

I'll have a faith that is mature.

I'll be close to God and faithful.

With Him forever, safe and secure.

—Elaine Kennelly

Oh, _____, It is by grace you have been saved, through faith. It is God's gift to you, but I want your faith to grow, and I desire an intimate relationship with you. Remember, the Kingdom of God is like a mustard seed that grows into a mature tree. Continue to ask, seek and knock. I am always listening for you.

Jesus

Sandra and "Cookie" are Elaine's Southern-speaking friends. "Bless Their Hearts". (2012)

Day 23
To Lament

as Christians, we can look forward to an eternity with some of the people we have met in the Bible. Did you ever think of that? Who would you like to meet?

One of the first I'd like to spend time with is Jeremiah ... the prophet from the Old Testament. Why him? Read his book and you'll be amazed.

Jeremiah was called by God to tell the Israelites bad news: Israel was going to be destroyed by the Babylonians and taken into captivity. Jeremiah urged them to repent and come back to God, but they never did.

Imagine, for Jeremiah a career of forty-one years of antagonism, even severe aggression, to the point of death. But Jeremiah persevered. He preached a message of God's judgment but also told of God's mercy. He endured and was faithful to God's call.

Why do I want to talk to him? I want to know how he did it.

Jerusalem fell in 586 BC. The city was burned to the ground, and its people were killed, tortured, or taken captive. Jeremiah's grief ran deep, and his tears were evidence of a broken heart. He was called the "Weeping Prophet."

The book of Jeremiah predicts the destruction of Jerusalem.

The book of Lamentations, also written by Jeremiah, looks back on the destruction of Jerusalem. It is really a funeral dirge in which he mourns for his homeland.

Have you ever had a broken heart? A really devastating time of sadness? A deep hurt that crushed your spirit?

Most of us have.

You will find affirmation of your sorrowful feelings in the book of Lamentations, as in "Misery Loves Company."

But then we get to the middle of chapter 3, starting at verse 19.

> The thought of my suffering and homelessness is bitter beyond words. I will never forget this awful time, as I grieve over my loss. Yet I still dare to hope when I remember this: the faithful love of the LORD never ends! His mercies never cease. Great is His faithfulness.
>
> His mercies begin afresh each morning. I say to myself, "The LORD is my inheritance; therefore, I will hope in Him!" The Lord is good to those who depend on Him, to those who search for Him. So it is good to wait quietly for salvation from the LORD. (Lamentations 3:19–26 NLT)

To lament is to mourn, to grieve deeply. Jeremiah is a good example for us. He openly weeps over his pain and distress. He struggles with it.

Sometimes I think Christians feel they must always be strong, facing up to fears and grief with a stiff upper lip, because God wants us to be strong. After all, He is a God of power. Yes, He is, but He is also a God of tender feelings, a God of deep compassion and mercy, who wants us to come to Him with our afflictions, our fears, and our deep sorrow. Jesus understands pain. After all, He suffered in so many ways.

Something Sisters, you may think God never hears you, and He is far, far away.

Or you may have shut Him out, casting aside His solace, never wanting to talk to Him again.

Either way, God still loves you. He is faithful, and His mercies are new every morning. But you may not realize that now, just like Jeremiah did not see the mercy and faithfulness of God until *He looked back.*

Prayer

Oh, my dearest Jesus, I am hurting, and I know not what to do. I am weak from my pain, and sleep does not come easily. I mourn for my loss, and I lament in my sorrow. I feel abandoned and empty. There is no one with whom to cry, so I will cry with You.

Have mercy on me, Oh, Lord. Look to me, and fill me with Yourself, for You are love and mercy, and I desire You with my entire being. I desire Your solace and Your peace, even though at times I am angry with You. Do not delay, for I am in need of You and Your comfort.

Thank you for Your Word in which there is judgment, horror, and death but also life, light, mercy, and grace. I love You, dearest Jesus. Come into my heart and into my life forever. This lamentation will end ... and then ... joy will come in the morning. You are a faithful God. Great is Your faithfulness. Amen.

The Music of the Soul

Tucked in the part of the Book, we call Old,

Is the Book of Songs and Rhymes, I was told.

It became my desire, searching for it was my goal,

To find what people called the music of the soul.

I heard these haunting melodies had power to heal,

And all of the words were by God revealed,

That through the ages they had touched men's hearts.

They would enter one's mind and never depart.

The music of the soul became my purpose, my fate;

Would I never stop searching? Was I already too late?

I took hold of the Book, read every sentence, every word,

But I could not hear it—I thought it absurd.

God spoke, "My Music of the Soul" can only be found

Through suffering and anguish and pain, it abounds.

If you wish to hear healing sounds from your soul,

You must let tragedy take its heavy toll."

"Oh, yes," I said quickly, "my faith is strong and secure.

I can handle all problems and pain, rest assured."

Life went on near perfect, a marriage, two boys.

The music faded in the daily addiction to noise.

Then one day, it was in the Spring of the year,

My eighteen-year-old son died; a tragedy severe.

My soul was anguished; I felt God disappeared,

And coldly left me with a soul that was seared.

Nothing helped—no words, no person, no mate

Could assuage my bitter moments of anger and hate.

I felt totally alone, without any solace or peace,

And then, oh so softly, a chord of music released.

From the depth of my soul appeared a melody so soft,

And when it occurred, my heart carried it aloft.

It was as though the angels their song did extol;

I wept. I heard ... the comforting music of my soul.

"The Lord is My Shepherd, I am never in need.

He makes me lie down; in His pastures I feed.

God leads me inside a pathway of peace,

He renews my soul; He does His guidance increase.

Even though I walk through the valley of death,

His Presence is near me as I take every breath.

God is My Shepherd, I fear no hurt, no harm;

Courage comes as I see the power of God's arm.

He prepares a banquet for me, as my enemies look on.

Anointing my head with oil gives joy all along.

God assures me my life with His goodness grows,

And I know, without a doubt, my cup overflows.

Certainly goodness and mercy will stay close to me!

As God gives me strength and the freedom to be

Forever in His House to live and remain.

Forever His child and by His Love sustained."

As I had hoped, the music of my soul appeared

To provide its power to heal my pain and my fear.

I learned, at last, that my God is more than sufficient

To meet all my needs. His music is brilliant!

Elaine Kennelly

Dear _____, I really am on your side. My plan for My human creation was to live in a perfect garden forever, but then sin showed up through Adam and Eve. But I am a faithful Savior. Even though your heart may be breaking, I am right there next to you and in you to provide all that you need. Open your heart and receive.

My love forever, Jesus

Day 24
Hope and a Future

I sn't it just like God to put a surprise verse in the middle of one of His books. In the book of Jeremiah, we encounter the weeping, the warfare, the whittling-down of Jerusalem. And then we approach Jeremiah 29:11–14 (NIV).

> "For I know the plans I have for you, declares the LORD, plans to prosper you and not to harm you, plans to give you hope and a future. Then you will call upon Me and come and pray to Me and I will listen to you. You will seek Me and find Me when you seek Me with all your heart. I will be found by you," declares the LORD.

Jeremiah was written in the Hebrew language, as was all of the Old Testament, while the New Testament was written in Greek. Many years ago, I heard Charles Swindoll, through his radio ministry *Insight for Living*, speak about hope. He said that the Greek word for hope is *elpis.*

Three guesses as to how I remembered this for twenty-five years. Elvis, of course! Here is the note I wrote in my Bible regarding hope.

> Elpis means the desire of some good with expectation of obtaining it. The biblical concept of hope is a positive outlook toward an expected end. Not what might happen but what MUST happen.

In our culture today, we have a very different meaning for the word *hope*. "Oh, I hope those pair of jeans will still fit." "Oh, I hope the Green Bay Packers will win today." (Remember, I lived most of my life in Wisconsin. Go Pack!)

God is never wishy-washy. When He uses the word "hope" any place in the Bible, He means *it will happen.* He does not taunt us with hope.

In the middle of the siege of Jerusalem, God gives this beautiful gift.

> Jeremiah, tell everyone this great news: I am planning to prosper you, not harm you. In fact, I want you to know right now, that you can count on a future with Me. You will pray to Me, and I will listen to you. You will seek Me with all your heart, and guess what? You will find Me! (paraphrase by Elaine)

It breaks my heart when I hear TV preachers who use this Jeremiah passage to preach prosperity. "Just hang in there; God will send the money. The checks are in the mail!" Yuck!

This passage is not about riches; it's about relationship. God always desires relationship with us.

Dear Something Sisters, God is promising us a glorious gem of truth. If you seek God with all your heart, you will find Him. He says, "I will be found by you."

Remember when you played hide-and-seek with your toddlers? You would hide, but where did you hide? Was it someplace where you knew they would never find you? N-o-o-o! You hid where they would find you easily, and after they did, you both would scream with delight, hug, and do it all over again. Right?

I know some of you, dear friends, are hiding from God. You've been suffering, and it seems so unfair to you. Your daughter is a young mother, and she has been diagnosed with cancer or a rare disease. Maybe you just lost your husband. Maybe you've had an adult child move back into your home. Perhaps your mom has Alzheimer's, and she doesn't recognize you anymore. Maybe your teenage children or grandchildren are making poor lifestyle choices.

Or perhaps you have been hiding from God your whole life, always searching but never committing.

Here is God's promise to you: "I have plans for peace and not disaster, plans to give you a future filled with hope ... When you look for Me, you will find Me, when you wholeheartedly seek Me" (Jeremiah 29:11 GWT).

Here is another great verse with hope for your future. "For the eyes of the LORD range throughout the earth to strengthen those whose hearts are fully committed to Him" (2 Chronicles 16:9 NIV)

Hope for the Christian is what must happen, because God decreed it. Seek God through prayer. Seek God through reading His Word in a quiet place, where you can listen to Him answer you. Seek God through a Christian friend. Seek God through a Christian counselor or a pastor. Seek God through our website, *www.SomethingSisters.com*.

He promises you He will be found. Remember, He's not hiding in a difficult place.

Prayer

Oh, Glorious God, Thank You for all of the wonderful promises You give to us. Your prosperity includes forgiveness, love, and peace in our lives. I long for peace in my life, and I do seek You to find it.

I have been hiding, because sometimes I don't understand Your ways. Why does life have to be so difficult? Why do some get healed and others die? Please help me to throw away all those doubts and questions. Give me Your power to seek You with all my heart! I want to trust You more. I need to understand Your great love for me.

Then, when I find you, would You please bless me with a relationship that is steadfast, staunch, and stable? Give me strength, because my heart is fully committed to You. I love You, Father, and desire to please You.

In the name and power of Your Son, Jesus Christ. Amen.

Hope and a Future

God knows the plans He has for me.

They will cause me no alarm.

For God declares most faithfully,

His plans will do no harm.

Instead, He plans to give me life

To rely on Him to cope.

It will not be so impossible,

For He has promised hope.

He plans for me a future, but

Down His path I must pace.

All honor goes to Him alone

He has given me His Grace.

Something Sisters

I must call upon Him now,

And come to Him in prayer.

He promised me He'd listen;

He has promised me His care.

I must Him most deeply seek!

In His Word, He is found there.

Yes, I will find you Lord, today,

Through worship, Word, and prayer.

But I must seek with all my heart.

No portion can I keep.

I must surrender everything.

Then, He will prosper me with peace.

—Elaine Kennelly

_____. I promise I will let you find Me, when you seek me with all your heart. Know that I am waiting to strengthen you because I love you very much. You are mine! Eternity with Me is My precious promise to you, and it will never change because I am the same, yesterday, today and tomorrow. Come to Me today.

Jesus

Day 25
Another Polar Event

*L*adies, here we have the second installment of polar events. I found another glorious definition of oxymoron: "A rhetorical figure in which an epigrammatic effect is created by the conjunction of incongruous or contradictory terms."

Just in case you were slightly confused about the last definition in Day 16.

I also collected a couple more oxymorons that I really like

- Found missing
- Sanitary landfill
- Intense apathy
- Twelve-ounce pound cake
  (my favorite)

This *valuable information* was found at: *www.oxymorons. com/oxymorons.html.*

I thought sensitive guy and marital bliss were great, too, but for some reason, Tom did not think I should include them. Go figure.

Here is my second biblical polar event. You cannot *be grouchy* and *give gratitude* at the same time.

Just so everyone understands, my list of "grouchy" includes grumbling, whining, complaining, crabbiness, bellyaching, and kvetching.

Now what does God have to say about that?

He doesn't like it.

The book of Exodus wins the prize for the most grumblers, groaners, and complainers. No surprise there. Trekking forty years in the desert might cause a little grumbling. Of course, it was their incessant grumbling about the Promised Land that led God to keep them wandering in the wilderness.

Now this is really true—you can make all the choices you want, but you cannot choose the consequences.

What did Jesus have to say about grumbling? "Stop grumbling among yourselves" (John 6:43 NIV). This was spoken to a crowd listening to Him teach.

For me, the most convicting verse is Philippians 2:14 (NIV): "Do everything without complaining or arguing." All-inclusive wording again. It's very simple to understand the meaning of "everything." (And I didn't even have "arguing" on my list.)

First Peter 4:9 (NIV) says, "Offer hospitality without grumbling." James 5:9 (NIV) adds a caveat. "Don't grumble against each other, brothers and sisters, or you will be judged. The Judge is standing at the door!"

Gratitude is the opposite of grumbling. Grumblers are not appreciative people. Grumblers see what's missing, what God has not given them. People who are grateful see what God has given them, and they thank Him.

Gratitude in all circumstances brings you into the presence of God. "You touch God's heart" is an earthly way of saying God is very near to you. He desires to hear your thanks, praise, and appreciation instead of your grumbling and complaining.

They truly are incompatible. You simply cannot feel grateful and grouchy at the same time. Impossible! They both carry emotional feelings that cannot be conveyed physically at the same time. Try it—it's funny!

Consequently, gratitude is a cure for grouchiness. What have people said for centuries? "Count your blessings." I would take it a step further. Thank God all through the day for your blessings, and you will not have time to be grouchy or irritable.

Here's another challenge for you. Read the entire book of Psalms. Write down every verse that directs you to thank God. You'll have a lifetime of prayers that thank God for everything.

Here are more encouraging words from God.

> You received Christ Jesus the Lord, so continue to live as Christ's people. Sink your roots in Him and build on Him. Be strengthened by the faith that you were taught, and overflow with thanksgiving. (Colossians 2:6–7 GWT)

> Thank God that He gives us the victory through our Lord Jesus Christ. (1 Corinthians 15:5 GWT)

> Give thanks to the LORD, for He is good! His faithful love endures forever. (Psalm 107:1 GWT)

> Always thank God the Father for everything, in the name of our Lord Jesus Christ. (Ephesians 5:20 GWT)

Go back to "Day 21: A + N + B = God's Will."

Go for it!

Prayer

Praise the Lord!

Father, we lift up holy hands to worship You, praise You, and thank You for all things. You are so worthy of our praise. We sing praises to You. We abide in Your presence, for You are the giver of all gifts, including the gracious gift of salvation, the *best* gift of all. Thank You, Jesus, for dying on the cross for me. We have victory in Jesus and can rest assured we are forgiven all of our sins.

In weakness, when I complain or grumble over someone or something, please remind me of my own shortcomings. Help me each day to praise more and grumble less. I do not want to be a negative person. Instead, I want to be filled with love, thanks, and appreciation for You, Father, and for my life. I am blessed beyond compare!

Keep my heart and mind in Christ Jesus! Amen.

Attitude? It's Up to You!

I'm sitting on my back porch, soaking up the sun,

Wondering why some folks are crabby and some are really fun.

What makes a person crabby? What's inside their brain?

They see their glass half empty. They even like to complain.

146

Something Sisters

Crabby people do not see their life being blessed by God.

They fail to appreciate. They think their life is flawed.

Joy passes right before their eyes, but they do not discern;

The minutes of their life go by, that can never be returned.

Time is the great equalizer of all who live on earth.

We only have the time to live, given to us at birth.

So every moment you are grouchy, harsh, or cross,

You've thrown away your time, and that's a terrible loss!

You'll never have that time again. No—forever it is gone.

When your mood turns crabby, may this light upon you dawn.

Count your many blessings and choose the path of Joy.

Shut out all the grouchy thoughts, your anxiety destroy!

Now enjoy today and all that you've been given.

Choose to think in positives. To Joy you will be driven.

Your attitude is up to you. Every day you make the choice

To be crabby or be happy. Let Joy be in your voice!

Then you will see a difference in your life from day to day.

For Joy will always bless you. Put it in your heart to stay!

—Elaine Kennelly

My dear _____, when you continually thank Me, you join people all over the world who are praising Me in word and song. It's My earthly choir that joins My heavenly choir, and the praise is a sweet fragrance to Me. *You* become a blessing to *Me!*

Love, Jesus

Diana and Elaine shared an office together at Keller Williams Realty. You really can have fun at work! (2012)

Day 26
When Jesus Comes Again

*J*am so excited! Today I am sharing one of my all-time favorite Bible verses with you, my friends. It's about overcoming.

Are you an overcomer? Have you triumphed over any of these in your life:

- A great sadness

- An extremely difficult situation

- A debilitating disease

- A time of severe testing in your life

You are an overcomer if you can answer yes to any of the above.

We who have suffered and overcome are part of a multitude of women warriors who will reap their reward when Jesus comes again. But we can also live victoriously here and now.

We can have joy in our lives again.

If you, sweet Something Sisters, are in tumult, trouble, or sadness right now, let me give you hope.

- Keep persevering. In other words, hang in there!

- Stay close to Jesus in daily devotions.

- Read your Bible every day, and pray honestly to God.

- Search out Christian friends who will help you.

- Read Christian inspiration at *SomethingSisters. com*.

Here is my favorite verse.

> To [she] who overcomes, I will give the right to sit with Me on My throne, just as I overcame, and sat down with My Father on His throne. (Revelation 3:21 NIV)

Come and see the picture I am painting for you.

There is a shock in the air—the commanding shout from the archangel! The trumpets are blaring, and Jesus is coming to earth, just as He went up to heaven with simple majesty and mighty authority.

The King cometh!

Those who have already died are coming out of their graves … miraculously! I watch them walking, completely whole and beautiful. Even if ashes were scattered or the depths of the ocean took their bodies, they are alive! They greet their loved ones with gaiety and gladness, and there is awe in every face. They know what *this* day means. They have been waiting.

Oh, look … there … I see my best friend, Betty, resplendent in her robe of white. I lost her so many years ago. Look, she is dancing over to me with my childhood friend Judy, who passed away just recently. We join hands and lift them up to praise Jesus. We are dancing and cheering, "Hurray for today! Hurray for today!"

And then my eyes meet Matthew. We embrace with all the love we have for each other. Every one of my loved ones is here. There is joy and celebration everywhere!

The music is majestic, and the angel choirs are praising God. I always feared the return of Jesus would be chaotic, but a peaceful rejoicing has spread across the horizon for as far as I can see. Exuberant people are everywhere; laughter rings in the air. I have never experienced such exciting energy.

Look ... there in the clouds ... I see Him ... It is Jesus, the Light of the World. Golden and brilliant and stunning—yet it does not hurt my eyes to look at Him. All His children are worshipping Him, praising Him, thanking Him.

Something is happening. My feet do not feel the earth. We are ascending, just as I always imagined. I am rising, ever so slowly, above the billowing clouds, above the breeze, ever rising, ever looking to Jesus. Singing to Jesus, "Worthy is the Lamb."

A throng of people envelops the entire space I can see. There are more than could ever be counted. People are from every nation, tribe, people, and language.

It is heartwarming to be home. Jesus walks to His magnificent throne and sits down next to His Father. They join hands, and majesty fills the air. "Hallelujah! Salvation and glory and power belong to our God," comes the roar from the multitudes, "for true and just are His judgments."

Soon after, a soundless hush begins to engulf all of heaven. It ripples down to where I am standing. We are all in the perfect stillness of God ... and Jesus looks in my direction.

He smiles softly and gazes at me attentively. His eyes are electrifying. His face is as glorious as the morning sun, flooding the horizon at the first second of the sunrise. He lifts His arm, and with a sweep of His dazzling robe, His hand is open. I see the scar from the stake pounded into his hand ... and ... there is something else ... There is a name engraved on the palm of His nail-pierced hand. It starts with an E ... then L ... then A ...

Why, it's *my* name on His tortured hand, and tears tumble down my face ... tears of joy ... tears of love ... tears of promises fulfilled. Jesus lifts His hand and motions for me to come forward. I am not frightened, and I move deliberately and gradually toward my precious Jesus. The crowd parts as I make my way toward His throne.

The heavens are hushed. Jesus smiles and speaks lovingly to me, and all can hear, "To you, Elaine, who have overcome, I give the right to sit with Me on My throne, just as I overcame and sat down with My Father on His throne."

He gently lifts me, kisses my forehead, puts me on His eternal throne, and sits down next to me. All the pain, sadness, and suffering are forgotten. Overcoming was my decision, made in the heat of battle. Being victorious is God's gift, given in the presence of His glory.

> Who is it that overcomes the world? Only [she] who believes that Jesus is the Son of God. (1 John 5:5 NIV)

Prayer

Dear Jesus, my holy God, how magnificent is Your glory, Your power, Your love for Your children!

I can hardly wait for Your return, or my passing from the earth into the heavenly realms. The great blessing is that *all* people have the opportunity of heaven given to them—*all* who believe Jesus is the Son of God, that He died in our place, will be welcomed home to heaven.

Thankfulness certainly fills my heart, Jesus, and I want each day of my life to reflect that thankfulness. I want to become more like You, Jesus. I want to grow in faith, in godliness, in kindness, in giving away what I have.

I want to share this good news with others around me. I want to share my earthly blessings with others who have less than I do. I want to encourage others, pray for others, and love others just as You love us.

Send Your Spirit, Your power, to accomplish all that You desire for me to accomplish. Then I will overcome any obstacle!

All my love and thankfulness, in Jesus' name. Amen.

She Who Overcomes

For years there was a battle raging in my heart and mind;

I could not understand My Jesus. I always pictured Him as kind.

Where was God, with all His blessings of love, health, and peace?

Where was the God I thought was love? For me, it had ceased.

A fierce battle was being fought in the very depths of my soul.

Why must I endure such sadness … my own personal hellhole?

I was losing the battle … my heart becoming bitter and hard;

I flung myself prostrate, giving up myself and my guard.

I sobbed, pounded fists, "Papa, give me the courage to win."

I then let the solace of God's love and peace finally come in.

"I need You to take over my thoughts. With pain I'm overrun.

Do you still love me, dear Papa? I want from guilt to overcome."

God's relief did not come instantly, just a little more each day.

I felt that God's presence was returning in many new ways.

From the Bible came power; God made me strong and bold.

The Spirit loved me, guided me away from my evil stronghold.

At church, I was teaching children again; I gave myself away.

I found that in sharing myself, joy returned without delay.

"I'm an overcomer! I'm victorious over guilt, grief, and sin.

Through the power of Jesus, I'm whole—at peace from within."

—Elaine Kennelly

My treasured _____, focus your life on Me, overcoming all your pain, and you, too, will sit with Me on My throne. Trust that I am preparing a place for you. Remember My hope for you—not that it might happen, but that it *must* happen. I will be there when you come home, or I will come to take you home.

Love, Jesus

Day 27
Trust Training

*H*ere is the plain truth:

- We will never grow in our relationship with God.

- We will never grow in our faith.

- We will never fall more deeply in love with Jesus.

If we do not learn how to trust Him wholeheartedly.

God's goal for today is to learn some trust how-to's. Think back to your Sunday school training or to an adult Bible class. Did you ever receive a handout that read, "The Process of How to Trust Jesus More"?

Today you will.

We Christian women, who are not new believers, have ample theology. We have heaps of head knowledge. We know the basic tenants of our Christianity. We are book smart.

We've learned what but not how. Today we are going to tackle the how.

This is not an easy task. Trust develops over time, and when life is humming along relatively well, trusting God is not a big issue.

But when adversity strikes? Do you know how to trust God?

I would like to encourage you today, dear friend. God has all the answers to every problem and to every situation. Let's learn together.

Encouragement from Elaine

1. *Remember Jesus loves you.* I have a surprise for you—adversity can question, diminish, or even wipe out the love of Jesus for you and your love for Him. Here's how to overcome.

- Memorize Psalm 18:1 (NIV): "I love you, O LORD, my strength." Say it over and over. Whisper it. Shout it. Sing it. You may not *feel* like loving Jesus, but you know you love Him. He loves you; He gave His life for you! Remember John 3:16.

- Your mind is powerful, but emotional feelings are "iffy." Trust God by staying in relationship with Him through love. Not only do you love Him, but with this short verse, you are honoring the fact that He is your strength.

2. *Remember that Jesus has authority over everything.* We are not always capable of perceiving the big picture of God's ways. We can't make sense of it. It's often illogical and hurtful, but we *do* have the knowledge of Jesus' supremacy. He is King of Kings and Lord of Lords! Here's how to overcome.

- Memorize Job 1:21b (NLT): "The LORD gave me what I had, and the LORD has taken it away. Praise the name of the LORD!"

- Say it to yourself over and over. Praise the name of the Lord. You cannot worry and worship, remember?

3. *Pray always and then do what you have to do under God's guidance.*

- When Nehemiah and company were rebuilding the Jerusalem wall, they heard about a life-threatening plot to destroy the Hebrew families that had returned.

- Let's make this personal. You and your family permanently leave the country, city, and home you have lived in all your life. You feel guided by God, and you want to be obedient to Him. On this mission trip, you trust God to protect you and your family. After all, you are doing God's work.

- However, enemies emerge, and you, your husband, and children are literally "under the gun." What went wrong here? You wonder, *I am doing God's bidding, and now my entire family might be killed by enemy snipers.*

- Memorize Nehemiah 4:9 (NIV): "But we prayed to our God and posted a guard to meet this threat."

- When adversity strikes, you will have to create your "action item." Nehemiah posted a guard.

- Later, as things got worse, "Half of the men did the work, while the other half were equipped with spears, shields, bows and armor" (verse 16).

- "Those who carried materials did their work with one hand and held a weapon in the other" (verse 17).

- They prayed, over and over again, but did what they had to do. FYI: the wall was built in record time—fifty-two days!

Bottom line: when things are humming along well, *that* is when you need to work on trusting God. If you wait until disaster strikes or the can of "affliction worms" opens, or you are really in a difficulty, it is much harder to start your trust training.

Our pastor, Dr. Jimmy Jackson, taught us there are seven ways to voluntarily suffer for Christ:

- Holy Living — make Godly choices
- Praying — intercession for others
- Going and Doing — missions
- Giving — tithes and offerings
- Loving — others first
- Trusting Him — total surrender
- Forgiving — when you have been wronged

What he said was that we can "practice" suffering so that when the stuff we don't sign up for comes (cancer, death of a loved one, car accidents, and so on), we will keep the faith and be able to trust Jesus more easily. In other words, we can build up our trust training so that when we really need it, we'll be ready and stronger in our faith.

All seven of these actions listed above are bonding us with Christ, unifying our spirit to His, day by day.

Trust training starts now.

Prayer

Dear Jesus, I really am grateful that You are in control of everything, including my life. I admit that many times I have wanted the control but messed things up pretty badly. Forgive my lack of trust.

Give me Your Holy Spirit power to trust You when times are good and when calamity strikes, to love You through the sweet times and the not-so-sweet. I bow before Your authority and surrender myself to You.

Increase my prayer-life, and help me memorize Your words and thoughts in Scripture. I want more of You, dear Jesus, and more of Your love for me.

I love You in return and take great delight in being Your child.

In the trust-filled name of Jesus, I pray. Amen.

Relationships

It's all about relationship,

Me and God and God and me.

For God is in relationship,

Three in one and one in three.

His love is unconditional

A love that is unfailing.

His almighty power is mine.

His grace is all prevailing.

So, why then do I worry?

If His power He will give.

I must learn to trust in Him,

As I believe, so shall I live.

—Elaine Kennelly

My dear daughter, keep loving Me every day, and always remember that I love you very much. I am especially fond of you, _____. When trouble comes, and it will, remember nothing can separate you from My love. I will never leave you, and My strength is free.

    Jesus

Day 28
I Will Refresh the Weary

*J*s there anyone out there, Something Sisters, who is weary? I'd have fewer to count if I had asked, "Is anyone out there in the world who is *not* weary?" Not many.

What has happened in our culture? What has happened in our families, our jobs, and our churches?

Everyone is crazy busy. That phrase comes from a book by Edward M. Hallowell titled *Crazy Busy: Overstretched, Overbooked, and about to Snap.* He opens with a story about his family on vacation at a cottage with no cell phone service and an old rotary phone. He is about to explode at how long it takes to make a call when he times the dialing process to reinforce his thinking. Imagine this—it took eleven seconds to dial the number.

It took me less time than that to purchase the book in Kindle format. Honest!

We are obsessed, hooked, and under the influence of speed and busyness and noise in our lives today.

> Come to Me, all you who labor and are heavy-laden and overburdened, and I will cause you to rest. I will ease and relieve and refresh your souls.

> Take My yoke upon you and learn of Me, for I am gentle (meek) and humble (lowly) in heart, and you will find rest, relief and ease and refreshment and recreation and blessed quiet for your souls.

> For My yoke is wholesome (useful, good—not harsh, or hard, sharp or pressing, but comfortable, gracious, and pleasant), and My burden is light and easy to be borne. (Matthew 11:28–30 AMP)

Who wouldn't want an invitation like that? Well guess what? Today it's your invitation directly from Jesus.

We're going to use the journalistic approach: *Who? What? When? Where? Why?*

Who? Jesus is speaking. He had been teaching and preaching in the cities of Galilee. We're not sure how many cities He went to, but remember He walked everywhere.

People were always wanting something from Jesus—healing, release from demons, blessing their children, speaking in the synagogues, teaching on the hillsides. Plus He was pulling a team together called disciples. Whew!

I think Jesus was weary Himself. Remember, He was true God but also true man. His humanity allowed Him to identify with us. He got hungry, thirsty, sleepy, and frustrated. But He did not sin.

What? An invitation is being given. Come to Me all who labor. All who must work two jobs, who cannot retire for lack of funds, who are caregivers for aging parents, who have adult children moving back home, who are raising grandchildren, or who are raising a family all by yourself. Come.

Come to Me ... all who have burdens, who are in chronic pain, who are carrying around emotional baggage, who are burdened with emotional strongholds, who are lonely, grieving, or simply worn-out. Come.

Take My yoke ... partner with Me ... join Me ... be in relationship with Me. Jesus desires to be in a redemptive relationship with you. That is why He came in the first place. You are important to Him, and He is very fond of you! His yoke is comfortable, gracious, and pleasant.

Learn of Me ... I am gentle and meek. I am humble and lowly in heart. Jesus is not a tyrant who wants to torture you. No! He is your forever-loving Savior and friend. You can trust Him when you know how much He loves you. Learn about His gentleness, His humility, and His love.

When? The time is now. None of us knows how much time we have left. Some of us will die soon, and some will live to be a hundred. God says to us, "Now is the time of God's favor. Now is the day of salvation" (2 Corinthians 6:2 NIV).

Partner with Jesus today ... pray and ask Jesus right now to come into your heart and life. Ask the Spirit for faith now, before it is too late.

Where? It all starts in your mind and heart. We have the highest cognitive thinking process of all God's creatures. God gave us the freedom to reject His gracious invitation. A relationship with Jesus Christ starts with, "Yes, I need to be forgiven."

Why? I will cause you to rest. Jesus promises us relief, ease, refreshment, recreation, and blessed quiet for your souls.

This is the way Jesus works. He desires to bless you with quiet for your soul. Can you relate to that? Oh, I know you can! Everyone in our country is begging for peace, for quiet, for relief, for rest, and recharging.

Jesus *is* the Way, the Truth, and the Life.

Prayer

Oh, Jesus, I want all of You in my life. I am in need of refreshment and rest, for I am weary, tired, and even afraid.

On some days, I feel I'm on the brink of not being able to hold myself together.

Come into my heart and my mind, and give me peace—Your peace. Please give me quiet for my soul. Ease the ups and downs of my emotional burdens, and give me an extra measure of Your love.

Give me relief from my intense busyness and my incessant planning. When I do that, I crowd You out of my day. Help me, Oh, Holy Spirit, to start my day with Jesus by giving Him my time, my mind, and my heart.

Yes, I am weary, and I want Your rest. In the name of Jesus. Amen.

Feelings

Sometimes I feel so empty, so very tired, and all alone.

My day is rushed. My needs aren't met. I'm weary to the bone.

Sometimes I feel so blue; I have so much sad inside me

I don't know what to do—there is no one here to guide me.

Sometimes I feel invisible—that life has passed me by.

I give and then I give some more, it makes me want to cry.

I am older now, but there are still those who daily need me.

My folks, my kids, my boss ... but none to emotionally feed me.

I have no peace, no joy, and I have feelings of unrest.

Ha! Who said your golden years would be your very best?

"I did," said Jesus Christ as He listened closely to my thoughts.

"I have all you need today. With My blood you were bought.

I saved you and give you countless blessings with My grace.

I bring My rest, relief, and joyfulness—a smile on your face.

Your busyness and your schedule have taken a heavy toll,

Come to Me, and I will give you blessed quiet for your soul."

—Elaine Kennelly

Dearest _____, I am relaxation, renewal, and restoration. I am all you need to be refreshed. Remember, even I stopped working on the seventh day, and I am God. Oh, you who are weary, come to Me for rest.

Jesus

Day 29
Do You Really Want More of Jesus?

*J*esus asked the invalid at the pool of Bethesda, "Do you want to get well?" (John 5:7). As a young woman, I couldn't understand the logic of the question. It was one of those "duh" moments. Of course, he wants to get well. He's been lying there unable to walk for thirty-eight years!

But the older I get, the more I see—especially in the Christian community—it is an excellent question ... one we need to answer.

Do you really want more of Jesus?

You see, some of us have been lying by the pool of our pride for thirty-eight years.

> You should know this [your name], _____, that in the last days there will be very difficult times. For people will love only themselves and money. They will be boastful and proud, scoffing at God, disobedient to their parents, and ungrateful. They will consider nothing sacred. They will be unloving and unforgiving; they will slander others and have no self-control. They will be cruel and hate what is good. They will betray their friends, be reckless, be puffed up with pride, and love pleasure rather than God. (2 Timothy 3:1–4 NLT)

Do you find yourself anywhere in that paragraph? Be honest, very honest, and truthful to God about this. It's *you* who is getting the evaluation here, not your children, grandchildren, spouse, neighbor, someone at work, or anyone at your church.

Now, write down what you have chosen. Write it on the inside cover of this book—and don't be arrogant—you're in that above paragraph. So am I.

Next, open your Bibles to 1 John 3:6a. Here it is in the Amplified Version.

> No one who abides in [Jesus], who lives and remains in communion with and in obedience to Him— deliberately, knowingly and habitually commits or practices sin.

In other words, if you profess to be in communion or in a relationship with Jesus, you do not deliberately and habitually keep on doing the same sins over and over and over again. Especially the sin we just wrote down, because, we are fully aware of these sins. The good news: if you are in Christ, your sin is forgiven. And let's also remember God has all the answers to every problem and situation.

Encouragement from Elaine

Hooray! You are the good seed that has fallen on good soil.

In Luke 8:11 (NIV), Jesus says, "The seed is the word of God." In verse 15 (NIV), He says, "But the seed on good soil stands for those with a noble and good heart, who hear the word, retain it, and by persevering produce a crop."

The word of God falls on you, the good soil. You have a noble and good heart. Notice it does not say you are sinless, but you do hear the word of God. You retain it. You persevere. You produce. Yea!

So do you want more of Jesus? Do you want to produce more for Jesus?

1. *Listen to and read the Word of God every day.* Don't study it. Don't read it out of obligation, don't check it off your to-do list. Just read it for the sheer pleasure of enjoying Jesus. Delight, revel, relish, and savor the Word. Let go, and delight yourself in the Lord. After all, He delights Himself in you! Read Psalm 18:19.

2. *Retain the Word of God every day.* That means you absorb it, you own it, you memorize it. Here we are again—memorize Scripture and put it away in your brain. Then every night before you fall asleep, repeat those precious words. When you open your eyes in the morning, repeat those precious words. When you are in trouble, when Satan is tempting you, or when you are doing something you know you should not be doing, repeat those precious words.

3. *You persevere, which means you will have problems every day.* Yes, something will happen every day to interrupt your wanting more of Jesus. I think, dear Something Sisters, at our age, we realize that it is all too true. You will have problems, but you will persevere!

4. *You produce a crop every day.* Intend to build a bigger crop, a crop of higher quality, a crop designed especially for you by Jesus. Let Him use you!

He may take you out of your comfort zone. He may give you a task way above your capabilities. He will have you encounter roadblocks along the way. He may put you "on hold." He may give you a task you do not like.

The exciting part? You will love Him more and serve Him better. In obedience to His Word, you can always have more of Jesus if that's what you really want.

Prayer

Dear Jesus, I am thankful to You for pointing out my pride to me and my reluctance to grow in my faith. It is essential that I grow. Please do not let me be a seed that grows up and is choked out by sin or by the worries in my life.

I do want more of You in my life, sweet Jesus. Today I make a commitment to read my Bible every day and delight myself in You. I have been reading the Bible in a year, and I must admit, I do check it off when I am finished. Please help me to enjoy You as well as learn from You.

Help me through Your power to produce a deeper faith. One that will withstand the troubles and temptations of this world, and one that will be thrilled to memorize and retain Your Word in my heart and mind.

With God all things are possible! I put my trust in You. Amen.

At My Kitchen Table

At my kitchen table, I meet Papa every day.

Precious words to me, He daily wishes to convey.

His protection surrounds me and those whom I love.

He keeps us all in perfect peace,

Then takes us home to heaven above.

Something Sisters

But if I do not come, or if I do not listen,

I have missed His blessings, and

His thoughts to me are hidden.

At my kitchen table, I meet Jesus every day.

I long to listen closely, for He has much to say.

He's my Shepherd, leading on the path made for me.

He's my all-sufficient Savior.

Forgiveness is fully guaranteed.

But if I do not come, or if I do not listen,

I have missed His blessings, and

His thoughts to me are hidden.

At my kitchen table, I meet God's Spirit every day.

He's my ever-present hope; He teaches me to pray.

He's my counsel, showing how to live life worry-free;

He's my inner rest and comfort.

He speaks His loving thoughts to me.

But if I do not come, or if I do not listen,

I have missed His blessings, and

His thoughts to me are hidden.

Something Sisters

At my kitchen table, it's the first place I will be.

Daily in His loving way, God speaks His heart to me.

He's the giver of all perfect gifts, and He loves us all.

In His presence you'll be blessed,

If you listen daily to His call.

—Elaine Kennelly

Dear _____, you may think My advice absurd, but take your day, and put your first hour away to read into your mind the power of My Word.

Jesus

Rachael and Elaine, crazy and full of laughter at work, at church, or wherever they go. (2012)

Day 30
On the Path of Life, Every Woman Needs a Something Sister

*J*t's the twentieth anniversary of the phrase, "Something Sisters." Two women performed a tap dance, and were introduced as "The Something Sisters 'cause they are really *something*."

It's one of those phrases that just pops into existence and, of course, sticks around. Maybe they really are *something*, but I can tell you, they remain best friends, because through the years, God has taught them something important.

On the path of life, every woman needs a best friend.

That's what a Something Sister is—a best friend. I hope you have at least one, and you are blessed, indeed, if you have more.

For three years, Jesus built a team of disciples. They were uneducated, middle-class, hardworking men.

But shortly before Jesus is arrested Thursday night in the garden of Gethsemane, He pours out His heart to this rag-tag outfit He calls His friends. Here's what Jesus said to His disciples in John 15:15 (NIV).

> I don't call you servants anymore, because a servant doesn't know what his master is doing. But I've

called you friends because I've made known to you everything that I've heard from My Father. You didn't choose Me, but I chose you.

I have a note in my Bible that says, "Jesus called His disciples friends, because He had disclosed His Father's revelation to them." When Jesus was transfigured, Peter, James, and John were there, witnessing the glory of Jesus. They saw Moses and Elijah.

They all had confidential access to Jesus. They were tutored privately by God (now think about that). They saw the miracles up close and heard every parable's explanation.

I'm sure they had funny moments, too. I can hear it now— stories, jokes, maybe even a few pranks.

God and the guys ... I don't mean that disrespectfully, but Jesus was true God *and* true man. It was a group of guys!

But when the crucial, critical, moment of truth came, they all ran. And Jesus wasn't even surprised. Then He willingly laid down His life for His friends.

My precious Something Sisters, learn from Jesus.

1. *Don't have unreal expectations of your friends.* They love you, yes, but they are not perfect, and neither are you. Jesus told His friends, "Love each other as I have loved you" (John 15:12b NIV).

Real friendship is a partnership ... a sharing ... a togetherness of like minds, ages perhaps, a genuine caring for each other ... listening ... giving of yourself in kind ways ... unselfishness ... and lots of fun. You enjoy each other's company, and you retain a relationship through the years.

2. *Forgive each other, as Christ has forgiven you.* Can you imagine how many times Jesus had to forgive these twelve troublemakers in three years? Countless.

I wonder how many arguments they had among themselves. Countless. I wonder how many times Jesus thought about firing them all! Countless—on His human side. Thank goodness for grace.

But look at the results. By persevering—by forgiving countless times—Jesus built the foundation of the universal church of all believers for all times.

God is in the miracle business!

3. *Repair the broken friendship; restore the hurt relationship.* If sin is inevitable, so is hurt. It will happen. Friendships will get wounded. Relationships will seem ruined. There will be heartaches, and sometimes it grows into bitterness, anger, or depression.

   Let me assure you, friendships can be mended. Relationships can be repaired and renewed. Go to *www.SomethingSisters.com* and read the story under "Mend a Friendship." It's real. It's my story.

   Let the Holy Spirit heal the hurts. Allow for mistakes. Think about this: a friend of twenty to forty years really cannot be replaced. We may not live that long!

   After His resurrection, Jesus restores His loving relationship with His disciples despite their desertion, disbelief, and denials.

   He miraculously appears to them. He lets them touch the nail print in His hand. He lets Doubting Thomas touch the spear scar on His side. He breathes the Holy Spirit upon them. Read John 20:22 (NLT).

   But there is one of the Twelve, one of the three most beloved, who grieves Jesus the most. It is Peter, who has been trained to be a leader. Is their relationship repairable?

   Jesus prepares a fish fry on the beach for His friends after supplying the fish in a miracle of multiplication. Jesus asks Peter, "Do you truly love Me?" Peter, listen up. "Do you truly love Me?" Simon, son of John, "Do you ... love ... Me?"

Three times! Oh, and Peter knows why He asked three times.

"Lord, you know all things. You know that I love You," is Peter's reply.

A relationship gone wrong is made right. Jesus forgives and sets the example for us. Note that the offended person, Jesus, makes the effort to reconcile the relationship with the person who was offensive. With us, we expect the one who was offensive to come and apologize first.

Just seek forgiveness and reconcile with your family and friends, no matter who starts the conflict.

Can you imagine how much Jesus loved the Twelve? Incredibly! But it is just as much as He loves you ... and your Something Sister.

Prayer

My precious Savior, thank you for being such an example for us. You could have turned Your back on all of us, but instead, You turned the other cheek. I am so appreciative.

My Something Sisters are my special blessings from You, and I thank You for their friendships in my life. Each one has touched my life in a very special and meaningful way. They are the sweet spirit that brings me joy and happiness.

I ask You, dear Jesus, to bless each friendship that is blooming on this earth today. Let them all grow into wonderful, long-lasting Something Sister relationships that bring You honor and glory.

Help us to forgive each other, love each other, and appreciate each other.

Bless us all to be a blessing to others. In Your miraculous name we pray. Amen.

Jesus Had a Friend

When Jesus started His public ministry,

He knew all about the team approach.

So very carefully He chose the dozen men

Who became The Team He would coach.

It tells us in the book of Luke, that

Jesus stayed up all night to pray.

God talked with God; the choices made.

Father blessed The Team that day.

There was Andrew, Peter, and Bartholomew,

James, the son of Zebedee, and his brother, John,

Thadeus, Philip, Matthew, and Judas.

Another James, Thomas, and Simon came along.

Three years went by. The time had come;

Jesus must give His life on the cross.

His Team was very frightened, unsure.

How could they ever bear the loss?

On the night of His final Supper

With His Team, He ate the Passover meal.

He then took them to Gethsemane.

He asked them to pray for His ordeal.

He asked The Team to stay with Him,

To pray for Him, and their watch to keep.

His soul was overwhelmed with sorrow,

But The Team just fell asleep.

Jesus was arrested in that garden,

Betrayed by a kiss prearranged.

How impossible for us to imagine such love.

It was Judas, He called His friend.

—Elaine Kennelly

Yes, you are My friend, _____, for you have everything I learned from My Father. I have given it to you. You did not choose Me, but I chose you. I have appointed you, so you might go and bear fruit, fruit that will last. This is My command: love each other as I have loved you.

Your friend, Jesus

Day 31
The Common Doxology

a doxology is a hymn that praises God. As a child, I often sang what we referred to as the Common Doxology. I think it was called common because everyone could remember it ... it was short!

Praise God from whom all blessings flow.

Praise Him all creatures here below.

Praise Him above ye heavenly host;

Praise Father, Son, and Holy Ghost.

Now *this* is easy to memorize! Sing it in the shower. Sing it in the car.

Praise is meant to be spontaneous! If you have the words in your head, you can even make up any melody you want.

It's between God and you, and there are no rights and wrongs. The most important thing about personal praise is the freedom you have to tell God how much you love Him. How good He is! How you appreciate His blessings. How you surrender everything to Him.

Sometimes I am so moved in my worship at home that I cry. Or I get down on my knees with hands uplifted, and I am overjoyed to the point of laughing. My worship is vibrant and dynamic. It is spirited and sparkling!

I love to worship and praise God, and I think that pleases Him.

Why do I think that way? Let's take a look at the best praise book around. It is found smack-dab in the middle of your Bible. It's called the book of Psalms.

Here you will find prayers and praise songs for every emotion. Let's take a look at some of my favorites from the Holman Christian Standard Bible.

> Be glad in the Lord and rejoice, you righteous ones; Shout for joy all you upright in heart. (Psalm 32:11)

> Turn to me and be gracious to me, for I am alone and afflicted. The distresses of my heart increase: bring me out of my sufferings. Consider my affliction and trouble, and take away all my sins. (Psalm 25:16–18)

> I will praise the Lord who counsels me—even at night my conscience instructs me. I keep the Lord in mind always, because He is at my right hand, I will not be shaken. (Psalm 16:7–8)

> God, create a clean heart for me and renew a steadfast spirit within me. Do not banish me from Your presence or take Your Holy Spirit from me. Restore the joy of Your salvation to me, and give me a willing spirit. (Psalm 51:10–12)

> For Your faithful love is as high as the heavens; Your faithfulness reaches the clouds. God, be exalted above the heavens; let Your glory be over the whole earth. (Psalm 57:10–11)

> I cry aloud to God, and He will hear me. I sought the Lord in my day of trouble. My hands were continually lifted up all night long; I refused to be comforted. (Psalm 77:1–2)

> Restore us, God of Hosts; look on us with favor and we will be saved. (Psalm 80:7)

> Your wrath seeps over me; Your terrors destroy me. They surround me like water all day long; they close in on me from every side. You have distanced loved ones and neighbors from me; darkness is my only friend. (Psalm 88:16–18)

> Take delight in the Lord, and He will give you your heart's desires. (Psalm 37:4)

Do you see the range of emotions? Wherever you are in your life, the book of Psalms will affirm you, comfort you, console you, invigorate you, nourish you, or allow you to sing your heart-out in praise to God. Plus it gives us solid biblical truth about God.

> The Lord is gracious and compassionate, slow to anger and great in faithful love. (Psalm 145:8–9)

> The Lord values those who fear Him, those who put their hope in His faithful love. (Psalm 147:11)

> Yet I am always with You; You hold my right hand. You guide me with Your counsel, and afterward You will take me up in glory. Who do I have in Heaven but You? And I desire nothing on earth but You. (Psalm 73:23–25)

> You are my shelter and my shield; I put my hope in Your word. (Psalm 119:114)

Take your Bible and a pen and go through every Psalm, yes, all 150 of them. Underline those verses that speak to you. Put a box around all those verses you love. Use different colored ink for different emotions. Let the book of Psalms be your praise and worship manual and your gripe and grief guidebook. It is meant to be all these things for us.

Here's one that pops into my mind when I feel like I am the underdog or perhaps God has just given me a challenge way over my head: "With my God, I can scale a wall (Psalm 18:29b NIV). Charge!

No, "Charge" is not part of the verse, but that is how I feel. I can picture myself going up, up, up, because I have my God with me. With His power working in me, I am invincible!

With God all things are possible. (Matthew 19:26 NIV)

Prayer

Oh, Almighty Father, thank You for the Bible, especially for the book of Psalms. You knew we would be very fragile creatures, who would need the affirmations and emotional support from Your Holy Book.

Thank You for the freedom to worship You in our homes, cars, churches. Take away our reticence to praise You loudly and with great emotion. Give us a vibrant spirit within us, a heartfelt spirit, a desire to worship You as the great God of the universe.

You are deserving of all praise, worship, glory, and honor. We love You and thank You for all of Your beautiful creation, Your gift of salvation, and Your spirit of sanctification.

You are King of Kings and Lord of Lords! We bow before You in humble adoration, knowing that through all eternity, we will enjoy You and delight in You. Praise God from whom all blessings flow. In Jesus' name. Amen.

You Are My Sunshine, Papa!

You are my *Song* every morning;
You're my *Stamina* during the day.
You are my *Shield* to protect me;
You're my *Strength* along the way.

You are my *Sunshine*, heavenly Father.
You are my *Sunshine*, Jesus Christ.
You're my *Sunshine*, Holy Spirit.
You're the *Brightest* of the bright.

You are *Security:* "In God We Trust."
You're my *Savior*—daily grace.
You're *Stability* for my busy life;
You're the *Smile* on my face.

You're my Salvation, I'm set free.
You are my Shelter in the storm;
You Satisfy my longing soul,
And then … You'll gently take me home.

Forever we will worship You.
Forever we will praise.
Forever we will love You,
And our hearts to You we'll raise!

—Elaine Kennelly

The Not-So-Common Doxology

Now, all glory to God, who is able to keep you from falling away, and will bring you with great joy into His glorious presence without a single fault.

All glory to Him who alone is God, our Savior through Jesus Christ our Lord.

All glory, majesty, power and authority are His before all time, and in the present, and beyond all time! Amen.

Jude: 24–25 NLT

Epilogue

*D*ear Something Sisters,

What a joy it has been for me to share Jesus with you! I am praying that you will seek forgiveness and peace through Jesus, and that you will grow stronger in your faith and daily life with Him.

Also, be praying for your special Something Sister friends. Perhaps one day we shall meet at a women's retreat, conference, or heaven, for sure.

Please feel free to go to our website, *SomethingSisters.com*, for additional devotions, affirmations, poems, and articles. There, you will also find free e-zine articles.

- "7 Letters to Eternity"

- "10 Daily Spiritual Affirmations"

- "Praying for Children & Grandchildren"

- "Something Sisters Share," our online newsletter

I want to leave you with a special Bible verse, one I love.

> Find rest, O my soul, in God alone; my hope comes from Him. He alone is my rock and my salvation. He is my fortress. I will not be shaken. Trust in Him at all times, O [Sisters]; pour out your hearts to Him for God is our refuge. (Psalm 62:5, 6, 8 NIV)

♥ *Elaine*

Journaling

Please use the space here for thoughts God gives you each day as you read, pray, and listen.

If you have never written down your thoughts during your devotion time, now would be a wonderful time to start. God will share His thoughts with you, but you must be in a quiet place to hear Him.

Be patient. It takes time, but the blessings that come from this discipline are priceless. God will speak to your heart and mind. Start today.

_____

_____

_____

_____

_____

_____

_____

_____

_____

_____

_____

_____